Look what people are saying about these talented authors....

Of Kate Hoffmann...

"Hoffmann's deeply felt, emotional story is riveting. It's impossible to put down."
—*RT Book Reviews* on *The Charmer*

"Romantic, sexy and heartwarming."
—*RT Book Reviews* on *Who Needs Mistletoe?*

Of Rhonda Nelson...

"Well plotted and wickedly sexy, this one's got it all—including a completely scrumptious hero. A keeper."
—*RT Book Reviews* on *The Ranger*

"Wonderfully written and heart-stirring, the story flies by to the deeply satisfying ending."
—*RT Book Reviews* on *The Soldier*

Of Tawny Weber...

"Sexy, hot, intriguing as well as fun are all hallmarks of a Tawny Weber tale."
—*CataRomance*

"If you like laugh-out-loud tales laced with spicy scenes, I recommend Tawny Weber. I look forward to reading more from this talented author."
—*Romance Junkies*

D0285516

ABOUT THE AUTHORS

Kate Hoffmann began writing for Harlequin Books in 1993. Since then she's published sixty books, primarily in the Harlequin Temptation and Harlequin Blaze lines. When she isn't writing, she enjoys music, theater and musical theater. She is active working with high school students in the performing arts. She lives in southeastern Wisconsin with her two cats, Chloe and Tally.

A Waldenbooks bestselling author, two-time RITA® Award nominee and *RT Book Reviews* Reviewer's Choice nominee, **Rhonda Nelson** loves dreaming up her characters and manipulating the worlds they live in. In addition to a writing career, she has a husband, two adorable kids, a black Lab, and a beautiful bichon frise who dogs her every step. She and her family make their chaotic but happy home in a small town in northern Alabama. She loves to hear from her readers, so be sure and check her out at www.readRhondaNelson.com.

Tawny Weber is usually found dreaming up stories in her California home, surrounded by dogs, cats and kids. When she's not writing hot, spicy stories for Harlequin Blaze, she's shopping for the perfect pair of shoes or drooling over Johnny Depp pictures (when her husband isn't looking, of course). Come by and visit her on the web at www.tawnyweber.com.

Kate Hoffmann,
Rhonda Nelson, Tawny Weber

IT MUST HAVE BEEN THE MISTLETOE...

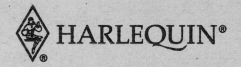

TORONTO • NEW YORK • LONDON
AMSTERDAM • PARIS • SYDNEY • HAMBURG
STOCKHOLM • ATHENS • TOKYO • MILAN • MADRID
PRAGUE • WARSAW • BUDAPEST • AUCKLAND

Recycling programs for this product may not exist in your area.

ISBN-13: 978-0-373-79583-3

IT MUST HAVE BEEN THE MISTLETOE...
Copyright © 2010 by Harlequin Books S.A.

The publisher acknowledges the copyright holders of the individual works as follows:

WHEN SHE WAS NAUGHTY...
Copyright © 2010 by Peggy A. Hoffmann

COLE FOR CHRISTMAS
Copyright © 2010 by Rhonda Nelson

A BABE IN TOYLAND
Copyright © 2010 by Tawny Weber

CONTENTS

WHEN SHE WAS NAUGHTY...

Kate Hoffmann

Prologue

THE WINDOWS OF THE converted school bus were caked with frost. Alison Cole peered out at the dimly lit parking lot. Though she loved winter, she'd always imagined it would be much more comfortable spent in a real home, with a fireplace and a functioning furnace and a Christmas tree with lights and tinsel—not in an old bus traveling the highways of...well, whatever state they'd found themselves in that day.

Today, they were at a holiday craft fair in Minot, South Dakota. Or was it North Dakota? Her musician parents were inside the arena, entertaining the crowds, while their three children were supposed to be doing the math homework their mother had assigned that morning.

Though her parents found this gypsy lifestyle fulfilling, Alison couldn't say the same for herself. A thirteen-year-old girl was supposed to experience certain things in life—boys, shopping, movies, school dances. She didn't even have a best friend, beyond eleven-year-old Layla and nine-year-old Rita. And who wanted to be best friends with their little sisters?

"That's mine!" Rita screamed.

Alison turned away from the window to see her sisters fighting over a fashion magazine. She broke up the argument and grabbed the offending article. "Where did you get this?"

Rita stared at her sullenly, refusing to answer, her arms crossed over her chest.

"She stole it," Layla confessed. "She found it on the counter at that diner where we ate dinner last night and she put it in her backpack on the way out."

"No one wanted it," Rita cried. "And it was just sitting there. They would have thrown it out anyway."

"Why would you want this?" Alison asked, flipping through the pages of *Vogue.* "It's for grown-ups, not little girls."

"I'm not little!" Rita reached out and grabbed the magazine. "Besides, I like the pictures. The models are…pretty. And the clothes are interesting. I'm making my Christmas list." She pointed to a photo. "I want these shoes."

Alison shook her head. "We should practice. I have a new song I want to try."

"We're supposed to do our math," Layla said.

In order to accommodate a life of touring, their mother had been homeschooling the girls at a table near the front of the bus. In addition to the basic subjects like math and history, the girls also got a large dose of traditional American music from their father—folk, country, bluegrass—along with a smattering of rock and pop. And all on their parents' collection of instruments—guitar, fiddle, mandolin, dulcimer.

When they weren't playing, they were listening, anything from Robert Johnson to Bill Monroe to the most obscure artists their father could find in the discount bin at the music stores they frequented. Alison had saved her meager allowance and made her first purchase a few years ago—a Jean Ritchie cassette she'd found at a flea market where her parents had been playing. From the moment she'd popped the cassette into the player, she knew this was her kind of music, simple mountain songs, full of longing and despair. This was the voice of an angel, and every day since, she'd tried to emulate it.

"Get your mandolin out, Layla. We can do math later."

Her sister eagerly scrambled over a pile of laundry that their mother had left for them to fold and grabbed the battered case of the mandolin she'd received the previous Christmas. Layla glanced over at Rita, who was now absorbed in her magazine, an anxious expression on her face.

Their youngest sister had never been interested in music. At only nine, she'd made it her goal to hate everything that Alison and Layla loved. She refused to conform to what anyone expected of her. She was stubborn and rebellious and a general pain in the butt. And yet, Alison still hadn't given up on her. If Rita had inherited any musical talent at all, it wouldn't take long to teach her what she needed to know.

"Skeeter, you have to sing, too," Alison said. She used her pet name for Rita, hoping she might persuade her sister to join in willingly. "This song really needs harmony and I can't sing both parts."

Rita rolled her eyes and sighed dramatically. "No. I'm reading. Make Layla sing."

"You're looking at pictures," Layla said. "And I can't sing and play at the same time."

"If you try, just for a little while," Alison said, "I'll get you another fashion magazine the next time we're in town."

"How are you going to do that?" Rita asked. "You don't have any money."

Alison wasn't sure how she'd keep her promise, but that didn't matter now. She'd heard an interesting song on one of her father's cassettes and was dying to try it out with her own little trio. The Cole Sisters. That's what they'd call themselves. Just like the Carter Family or the Judds. Since they were on the road anyway, why not become the opening act for their parents?

"I want to start with 'Barbara Allen,'" Alison said. "And then, 'The Cherry Tree.' And 'Gypsy Laddie.' And the new one is called 'Molly Ban.' It's so sad and pretty. It's about a boy who shoots his girlfriend because he mistakes her for a swan."

"Jeez," Rita grumbled. "What? Are you working up an act?"

"What if I am?" Alison glanced over at Layla. "It's not so impossible. Kid acts are really big and there are plenty of families who sing together."

"Yeah, when they're old," Layla countered.

"It's already been done," Rita said, her nose still stuck in the pages of her magazine. "They called it the Partridge Family."

"Who?" Layla and Alison asked in tandem.

Rita glanced up and sighed dramatically. "Some really old group from the seventies. The Partridge Family? They had a show on television."

"Mom doesn't let us watch television. When did you see it?"

"Those kids I met at the folk festival last fall," Rita explained. "They had a television in their bus and they had lots of tapes." She set her magazine down. "The show's about this family who rides around on a bus and plays music together. But they play rock music. And they have a regular house, too. And there's no father. And there are five of them and only three of us. Two, if you don't count me. And one if you don't count Layla."

"Next time you find someone with a television, you have to invite me along," Layla said. "When I get older, I'm going to have a television in every room of my house. And I'm going to eat as much candy as I want. And regular bread, not that whole wheat stuff that Mom makes us eat."

"So, what do you think?" Alison asked.

"About what?" Layla looked puzzled.

"A group. The three of us, together onstage. We could do it. We'd need to work on our harmonies, and Rita would have to learn to play an instrument, but if we perform together, we could make a little money."

Rita frowned. "Except that I *can't* sing or play or do anything that anyone wants to pay to watch. And Layla won't do it."

"Why not?" Alison turned to her middle sister. "You're the best musician of us all."

"She's scared," Rita said.

"I'm not," Layla countered.

"You are so. That time Mom and Dad brought us onstage last year at the Christmas show, you almost peed your pants you were so scared. And we were just singing 'Silent Night' along with them. You forgot the words and your face turned all red and then you had a stomachache for two days."

Alison looked at the stricken expression on Layla's face. "It's all right," she murmured, her dreams suddenly fading. "We can work on that. You'll get more comfortable the more you perform."

Layla shook her head. "No, I won't." She grabbed her mandolin and headed for the rear of the bus, then plopped down on the bunk bed she called her own.

Rita shrugged and went back to her magazine. "I guess you're just going to have to make a solo act," she said, a satisfied smirk curling the corners of her mouth.

Alison reached around her sister and picked up her dulcimer. "Well, Merry Christmas to you, too." She stomped up to the driver's seat and plopped down. "I hate this bus. I can never get far enough away from you two."

Someday, she'd have everything she dreamed about. Someday, she'd own a place—and it wouldn't have wheels! And she'd be the one making decisions about where she'd go and what she'd do. And when she performed, people would listen to her and smile and clap for hours on end. And when she traveled, she'd sleep in a proper hotel with a bed and a real bathroom. And when Christmas came around, she'd have a real tree, not some silly plastic thing they found at a flea market.

"Someday," Alison murmured. "Someday, everything will be different."

1

ALISON COLE PEERED OUT the rain-streaked window of her Subaru station wagon at the fork in the road. A quick glance at her GPS was no help at all. She'd been off the government maps for the past fifteen minutes.

She grabbed her cell phone from the seat beside her, determined to call Stephen, the graduate assistant who'd given her directions. But the moment she turned it on, she realized there wouldn't be service this far into the mountains. She punched in his number and waited, hoping that she was wrong. But when the call didn't go through, Alison tossed the phone back onto the seat.

The way she looked at it, she had two choices—well, actually three, if she counted turning around and going back down the road to civilization. "Right or left," she murmured. She had a fifty-fifty chance of finding Ettie Lee Harper's cabin. The same odds had her getting stuck on a muddy road with no way of calling for help.

Alison had spent the past four months tracking down the elusive Ettie Lee and she was running out of time. Her search had begun the moment she uncovered an old reel-to-reel recording in the archives at the university last summer. A yellowed label gave the date as 1939, but a sound technician friend said that the tape was probably a recording of an old phonograph record. It featured a young Ettie Lee Harper, her voice clear as a church bell on a cold winter night, singing Appalachian Christmas songs along with a dulcimer.

For a musicologist, it had been like discovering a treasure chest filled with precious jewels. Only Alison's jewels were songs—traditional songs that had been passed down for generations in mountain families and over time were transformed into entirely new versions. She recognized many of the original songs but there were three on the tape that were completely unfamiliar to her—three lost treasures that she was determined to uncover.

Alison had made Christmas carols the subject of her doctoral thesis at East Tennessee State, tracing the roots of Appalachian songs back to their origins with the Scots and Irish settlers who carved out a life in the Blue Ridge Mountains. Discovering a trio of new songs would open all sorts of doors. She could put together an album featuring the new songs or publish them in a folio. And she'd sing them at her Christmas-themed recital in two weeks.

The discovery alone was enough to assure her of her dream job, the chance to start a whole new department at the University of North Texas, one of the nation's top music colleges. The selection committee was coming to hear her Christmas faculty recital and she'd already been scheduled for a series of interviews in Denton.

With this new music, they'd have to see how important her work would be to their university. At the least, she'd finally get an offer of a tenure position at East Tennessee. She'd be Professor Alison Cole, Ph.D., making her music teacher parents proud.

"That's it," she muttered. "I'm calling the governor. This is ridiculous. I'm still in Tennessee. We have road signs in Tennessee."

Over the past year, Alison had ventured into the mountains

a number of times in search of singers and songs. And she'd learned one important thing—mountain folk were suspicious of outsiders. Maybe suspicious enough to pull down road signs? She leaned over the steering wheel and squinted into the gray light of the afternoon.

There it was. Not a regular Tennessee Department of Transportation sign, but a crude wooden marker nailed to a post. Alison jumped out of the car and ran toward it, trying to read the letters carved into the weathered plank. "Harper," she said with a smile. The left end of the sign had been fashioned into a point and she stared down the muddy road. Though the narrow cut through the forest looked nearly impassable, at least she knew there would be help at the other end if she got stuck.

Alison ran back to the car and got behind the wheel, then sharply turned the Subaru to the left. There were signs in the mud that another vehicle had passed that way recently, giving her a boost of confidence. After two minutes on the steep, winding drive, the thick forest opened into a small clearing. A pickup truck was parked off to the side of the driveway and she pulled in behind it.

A wide porch spanned the front facade of the rough-hewn log cabin and smoke curled out of a stone chimney. A small oil lamp flickered in the window between panels of a lace curtain. There were no wires or poles running along the driveway. Though indoor plumbing wasn't a must in many of the mountain cabins she'd visited, nearly everyone had electricity and phone service these days.

She honked her horn to announce her presence and waited for the obligatory dogs to appear to chase her off. When they didn't, Alison stepped out of the car and started toward the front steps. But halfway up the muddy path, the front door swung open. Two dogs came tearing out and Alison glanced over her shoulder, wondering if she could get back to the safety of the Subaru in time. Her split second of hesitation was too long and the hounds raced around her, barking and sniffing at her feet.

If that wasn't enough to frighten her, an elderly woman appeared on the porch, a shotgun in her hands. She raised it, pointing it directly at Alison. "You better watch yourself," she shouted, holding the gun steady. "This is private property and you're officially trespassing."

"There wasn't a sign," Alison called, protecting her eyes from the rain, which was slowly increasing to a downpour. "I'm sorry. I—I'm looking for Ettie Lee Harper. Does she live here?"

"There's nothing here for you. I don't have any antiques to sell, I'm not lookin' to buy life insurance and I don't wanna leave my savings to whatever charity you come callin' for."

A younger man appeared at the door and gently took the gun from the old woman's hands. They whispered something to each other and the woman nodded and went back inside.

"Just hop on back into your car and get on out of here before Ettie Lee has to shoot you," he said.

"So that was Ettie Lee." Alison took a step forward, then realized the man still had the gun in his hands. "I'm here about her music. My name is Alison Cole. From East Tennessee State. I heard her sing on an old recording and I wanted to talk to her about her songs."

Alison wiped the rain out of her eyes and pasted a friendly smile on her face as the man turned aside to discuss the matter with Ettie Lee. Though she'd met resistance before when speaking to mountain folk, Alison had never been on the business end of a shotgun.

A moment later, the elderly woman reappeared at the door and motioned to her. "Come on in, then," she called in a wavering voice. "I wouldn't wish this weather on my dogs." She cocked her head toward the man holding the gun. "Is she coming?"

"Yes, I believe she is, Miss Ettie."

"Is she pretty?" Ettie Lee shouted.

"Hard to tell, Miss Ettie. Right now, she looks like a drowned rat."

Alison stepped up on the porch and pushed the damp strands of her bangs aside, then sent the man with the gun a cool look. But the moment their eyes met, she realized that she hadn't seen much beyond the muzzle of the gun pointed at her. She swallowed hard as her gaze took in the details of his features.

He was beyond handsome, his eyes a piercing blue and his lips chiseled perfection. A day's growth of beard shadowed the planes and angles of his jaw and cheeks. Thick dark hair brushed the collar of his chambray shirt. When he smiled at her, she felt a shiver skitter through her body.

It had been so long since she'd had this kind of reaction to a man. Just last week, she'd been complaining about the lack of interesting men in her life over lunch with her best friend, Tess Robertson. Tess had warned her that the right man might come along at the most unexpected time.

She'd even presented Alison with a beautifully wrapped Christmas present—a box of condoms, insisting that they both needed to make a New Year's resolution to be a little more naughty and a little less nice.

Well, this man was certainly a surprise, as was the tiny thrill that raced through her when she met his gaze. All kinds of wicked thoughts rushed into her head. Maybe Tess had been right. At the most unexpected time and in the most unexpected place.

She tipped her chin up and gave him a coy smile. "You know what they say about men with big guns," she muttered.

"Come on inside," he said, arching an eyebrow as she passed. "We've got a fire going. You can dry yourself off and get warm."

DREW PHILLIPS CLOSED the cabin door behind the stranger and watched as she dripped water on Ettie's floor. Though he'd said she looked like a drowned rodent, his claim was far from the truth. Even soaking wet, Alison Cole was just about the most beautiful woman he'd seen in...in longer than he could remember.

He'd been trying to avoid looking at her since she'd arrived. There was something about her that he found so alluring, something that had caused his blood to warm and his pulse to quicken the instant their eyes met. She wasn't drop-dead, Hollywood gorgeous, the kind of beauty you found on the pages of magazines. Instead, she had a simple, natural beauty that even stringy wet hair and a lack of makeup couldn't diminish.

Drew groaned inwardly. Since he'd opened his practice a year ago, his sex life had been practically nonexistent. Making the decision to leave an urban hospital and move back to the mountain had been easy, but he'd never considered what the lack of available women would do to his libido. He'd just assumed that there would be opportunities, and if there weren't, he'd spend the weekend in town.

But there were always emergencies, people to look after, home visits to make, and the weekends slipped by without any break from his duties. All work and no play had made Drew a very horny boy. And now, with a beautiful woman standing nearby, his thoughts would naturally turn to sex.

"Why don't you get yourself out of that wet jacket," he said, placing his hands on her shoulders. He slowly pulled the garment off, the scent of her teasing his nose.

She shivered. "I—I'm a little cold."

Drew grabbed an afghan from the back of the sofa and wrapped it around her shoulders, rubbing her arms to warm her. His palms slipped to her back and he continued to massage her. "Better?"

She looked up and their eyes met. For a long moment, they stared at each other. He was so used to looking after his patients' well-being that it was only natural to try to make her more comfortable. But when he realized they were nearly embracing, he quickly stepped back. "Hypothermia can set in very quickly," he murmured.

It was obvious she'd been a bit shaken by the physical contact. When she spoke, her voice trembled. "Miss Harper, my name is Alison Cole. I've been searching for you for a long time." She held out her hand, a puzzled look coming over her face when Ettie didn't move.

Drew walked over to Ettie's side and took her by the elbow to lead her forward. "She wants to shake your hand, Ettie." He smiled at Alison. "Miss Ettie is blind."

"Don't say it that way," Ettie scolded in a deep drawl. "Tell her I just don't see things the way regular folk do." The old woman held out her hand and Alison took it in hers. "So you heard my recording? There was a man came by here last summer asking about those songs. Wanted to put them on a new record."

"Someone else knows about them?" Alison asked. Her expression fell and Drew wondered why the songs were so important to her.

"But I ran him off," Ettie continued. "Didn't like the sound of his voice. He came back twice, tryin' to get me to sign some papers, but you can never trust a man with papers."

"When did you record the songs?" Alison asked.

Ettie smiled. "My Lord, I remember that day like it was yesterday. It was 1939. My fourteenth birthday. And my daddy borrowed his friend's truck and drove Mama and me into Knoxville. It was the first time I'd been away from home and I thought I'd faint from all the excitement."

"You had a beautiful voice," Alison said.

"She still does," Drew commented.

Alison glanced over at him and his breath caught. Had he been staring at her this whole time? She was even more beautiful than he'd originally thought. He found himself undressing her in his head, discovering the body beneath the damp clothes.

He held out his own hand, challenging her to take it, to touch him. It was clear she was attracted to him. He could read the signs. "I'm Drew Phillips. I'm the doctor around these parts. I was just paying a house call to Miss Ettie when you came along."

The moment she slipped her fingers into his, Drew felt a current of anticipation race through him. It had been so long since he'd thought about a woman in a purely sexual way. Though he was considered quite a catch among his patients and their single female relations, Drew made it a point not to mix his professional life with his personal life. But this woman seemed as if she'd been dropped on this mountaintop for a reason—and maybe it wasn't just to talk to Ettie about her music.

"I like the sound of you," Miss Ettie said. "Why don't you two sit down near the fire and I'll get us all some tea? We'll have a nice chat." Ettie moved to the stove. "It's chamomile. I pick it myself."

"I'll do that," Drew offered, stepping to her side.

"No, no," Ettie whispered. "You throw a few more logs onto the fire and have a nice chat. She sounds like a very pretty girl. You could use a pretty girl in your life," she added, patting Drew on the arm.

Drew turned to face Alison, certain she'd heard everything Ettie had said. "Sit," he said, pointing to a chair near the hearth. "And don't mind her. She likes to play matchmaker whenever she can."

"Yeah, I can tell you probably have all kinds of problems finding women to date," Alison teased.

Drew chuckled. "I spend most of my free time with an eighty-five-year-old woman," he said. "That should tell you all you need to know."

"I wasn't asking," Alison said, tipping her chin up. "I'm not interested in you. Only Ettie."

"We're a package deal. I watch over her. If you take advantage of her, you'll have to answer to me."

Their gazes met again and Drew fought the impulse to lean forward and kiss her. He might have given in and done it if he could guess her response. But she watched him with a wary expression and he decided to wait.

"I—I need to get my recorder from my car. I don't want to miss anything she says."

"I can run out and get it," he offered. Maybe it would be best to leave her alone. After all, she'd come here to see Ettie, not to be the subject of his own personal sexual fantasies.

"Just bring the messenger bag from the front seat," Alison instructed. "That has all my things inside."

He grabbed his jacket from the chair near the door and glanced back at her, only to find her staring at his butt. She blinked in surprise and then blushed. Her pink cheeks said it all. She was having a few little fantasies of her own.

When he returned with her things, Alison rose from her spot near the fire and crossed the room. Their hands brushed as she took the bag from him. "Thank you," she said.

"No problem."

They stood so close their bodies were nearly touching. He could feel the warmth radiating from her and he found himself drawn to it, tempted to pull her into his embrace and enjoy the feel of her.

Alison wandered back to the fire and sat down, then began to rummage through her bag. "Have you ever heard Miss Ettie's recording? I have it on my iPod." She reached inside for the MP3 player and scrolled through the songs until she found what she was looking for, then handed it to him.

Drew held up the earbud and listened, adjusting the volume until he could hear clearly. He grinned as the older woman walked over to them. "Miss Ettie, you sound like an angel. So young."

"I was young," she said as she crossed to the fireplace, a tray in her arms. "And everyone wanted to hear me sing."

Alison stood and gently took the tea tray from her hands. "May I pour?" she asked.

Ettie sat down in her rocker across from them both and nodded. "Please do."

"Here, Miss Ettie," Drew said, handing her the iPod and earphones. "Put this next to your ear and you can hear yourself."

ALISON WATCHED AS DREW knelt beside Ettie's chair and held the earphones for her. He was so sweet and gentle with her, yet somewhere beneath that calm facade was a man who probably knew exactly how to please a woman in the bedroom. Alison saw it in the way he moved, in the way he looked at her.

She rubbed her arms, her thoughts going back to the wild sensations that had rushed through her when he'd touched her. She was glad for the digital recorder taping Ettie's words, because her own mind kept wandering back to Drew. He was, by all accounts, one of the most handsome men she'd ever set eyes on. And that she'd found him here, in the backwoods of Tennessee, was quite a surprise.

She hadn't really thought much about men lately. Her last boyfriend had walked away six months ago, a victim of her work schedule and an uninspiring sex life, and she hadn't been anxious to replace him. He'd been needy and bossy and intent on turning her into someone she wasn't—a woman happy to take care of him while he focused on his academic work.

But that didn't mean she'd put aside her desires. Right now, all that seemed to be running through her head were naughty images of Drew in various states of undress. With his shirt, without his shirt. She'd even found herself contemplating his choice of underwear—boxers or briefs?

As they sipped their tea, Miss Ettie commented on the songs she was hearing. At times, her eyes misted over with tears, or laughter bubbled from inside of her. Alison held out the recorder, capturing everything and asking questions along the way.

Every word Ettie spoke was a treasure, a new insight into the music that Alison had loved all her life. But as the afternoon wore on, she could see that Ettie was growing tired. Though she didn't want to call an end to their time together, Alison didn't want to overstay her welcome.

"I think maybe I have enough for today," she said when Ettie offered to brew a third pot of tea.

"No, don't be silly," Ettie said.

"She's right," Drew agreed. "You should get some rest. You still haven't regained your strength after being ill last month."

"Oh, I'm so sorry," Alison said. "I didn't realize you weren't up to this."

"I'm fine." Ettie waved her hand. "And there's so much more to talk about. You'll come back tomorrow."

Drew looked over at Alison and she nodded enthusiastically. "Yes, I think that would be best." She knelt down beside Ettie's chair and took her hand. "I'll come back. And I'll bring my dulcimer. Maybe we can sing together?"

Ettie smiled and nodded. "I'd like that, dear. Tomorrow. And you come back, too, Drew. I like having you both here."

"Tomorrow," Alison said.

She stood and picked up her things, stuffing them back into the messenger bag. Drew grabbed her jacket and held it out as she slipped her arms into it. He smoothed his hands over her shoulders, letting his touch linger for a long moment. Alison closed her eyes and leaned back into him. Then, catching herself, she slowly turned and looked up at him with a hesitant smile. "Thank you," she murmured.

"No problem." He called a goodbye to Ettie, then opened the door, stepping out onto the porch after Alison.

Outside, the rain was coming down in sheets. Though it was nearly Christmas, there hadn't been much snow. They stood next to each other on the porch, looking out at the weather. "Where are you driving to?" he asked.

"Johnson City," she said.

"This rain is bad. The road back to town might be washed out. Why don't I drive ahead of you until you reach the main road? Just to make sure you get out safely."

"All right," she said. In truth, she would have preferred that he just invite her back inside to wait until the weather improved. "But what if the road is washed out?"

"Then you won't be going back to town," he said with a shrug. He grabbed her elbow and pulled her along. "Let's go before it gets any worse."

Alison drew a deep breath and started toward her car at a brisk jog. But she hadn't got more than twenty yards from Ettie's cabin when she slipped on a muddy patch and felt her feet go out from under her. Before she could regain her balance, she landed on her backside.

Muddy water seeped into the seat of her jeans as she sat there, pain shooting from her ankle to her knee. "Ow," she cried, straightening the leg that had twisted beneath her. "Ow, ow." The strap from her messenger bag twisted around her neck and she pulled it off and clutched it to her chest.

In a heartbeat, he was beside her. "Are you all right?"

"I—I think I twisted my ankle," she said. She reached out to grab his arm, but her hands were covered with cold mud. "Help me up. I think I can walk."

"No." He scooped her into his arms, mud and all. "We'll go back inside."

"No!" Alison cried. "I'm fine, really. Just put me down. I'm not going to impose on Ettie, especially not covered in mud." He continued to hold her in his arms, his mouth just inches from hers, clouds of vapor from their breath mingling in the damp air. "I—I can walk," she assured him.

"I'm a doctor," he murmured, his attention focused on her face. "I'll know if you're lying."

"I think I can make it to my car," she said, waving him off. Wincing, she put weight on her ankle, then gritted her teeth and pushed through the pain. He held on to her arm as they walked to the Subaru. Her ankle throbbed as if it were about to explode and she felt her cheeks warm with humiliation.

But then, Drew gently grabbed her arms and drew her toward him. A moment later, his lips came down on hers, warm and searching for a response. At first, Alison was too surprised to move. But the next instant, she surrendered to the kiss, throwing her arms around his neck and pressing her body against his.

When it was finally over, he stared down at her with a surprised smile. "Follow me," he said, pulling the car door open for her.

Alison crawled inside and closed the door, then pushed her hair out of her eyes with her muddy hand. Her heart slammed in her chest and she found herself gasping for breath. Had that really happened? Had he just kissed her for no reason at all?

A few moments ago, she'd been ready to walk away from him, but now, she was prepared to stand in the pouring rain for just one more chance to kiss him. The heat from his lips was still fading as Drew's truck pulled up beside her. He honked the horn and drove ahead, waiting for her to turn around.

"Stop it," she muttered to herself. So he'd kissed her. It wasn't as if it had come completely out of the blue. They'd been lusting after each other all afternoon. It was only natural that he'd act on those feelings. And that she'd respond.

But this kiss wasn't just an ordinary kiss, Alison mused. The moment his lips touched hers, she felt something powerful rush through her body. Need. An aching need that couldn't be satisfied with only one kiss.

The car skidded and she was yanked out of her thoughts. It was raining so hard that she could barely see the taillights in front of her. She leaned forward and rubbed the fog off the windshield with her sleeve, leaving a streak of mud behind. Cursing softly, she tried to slip out of her jacket, but as she twisted in her seat, she saw the taillights flash in front of her. She slammed on her brakes, and the car skidded to a stop right behind Drew's truck.

A moment later, she saw him running toward her car. He jumped in the passenger side as she quickly threw her belongings in the backseat. Pushing back the hood on his jacket, he turned to her, little droplets of water clinging to his dark lashes.

"The road is washed out ahead. There's a big gully cut right across it. You won't be able to get through with your car."

"It's four-wheel drive," Alison said.

"Doesn't make a difference. You'll tear out the undercarriage and probably get so stuck it'll take a tow to get you free. We can try to go through with my truck, but I'm not sure even I can make it."

"What other choice do we have?"

"We can go back to my place and wait for the rain to stop," he said. "And then I can call someone in town to come out and fill in the road."

"Your place? You live up here?"

He nodded. "We just passed the turn about a hundred yards back."

Alison considered her options. Try to make her way down the mountain and spend the next couple hours, cold and covered with mud, driving through a rainstorm to get home. Or spend the evening with an incredibly sexy doctor, alone, in his mountain cabin. Should she waste energy thinking about it? Or simply admit that his offer was just about the most intriguing prospect she could imagine?

"If you think it best, then I guess we could wait out the storm at your place."

"Grab your stuff. We'll leave your car here and take mine."

"But what if someone hits it in the dark."

"Ettie and I have the only two cabins on this road," he said. "And she doesn't own a car. So I think you're safe."

Somehow, the word "safe" didn't seem to apply to being close to Drew. When she was near him, she felt that she couldn't think straight. And the kiss they'd shared. Maybe it would happen again, Alison thought to herself. Oh, who was she kidding? It would most certainly happen again. And after a few more kisses, they'd progress to other more interesting activities.

She swallowed hard and began to gather her things from the backseat. "All right. I think that would be best."

2

THE CABIN WAS COLD AND dark as Drew opened the front door for Alison. He circled around her and lit an oil lamp, which illuminated the rough interior. "I haven't spent a night on the mountain in a couple weeks. I usually stay in the apartment above the clinic." He lit another lamp. "It's rustic, but it's comfortable."

He watched her reaction carefully, a tiny sliver of guilt niggling at him. He'd seen the gully in the road. But maybe she could have made it across. There was a section that looked as if it might hold. Had he been quick to advise her otherwise because he wanted to spend the night with her?

Alison drew a deep breath and let it out, a cloud forming in front of her face. "It's cold."

"I'll get a fire started," Drew said, tugging off his damp jacket and crossing the room to the fireplace that dominated the west wall. "Take off that wet coat."

She was slender and long limbed, yet not very tall. And she moved with such a simple grace that he couldn't help but fantasize about the body beneath the soggy clothes.

"I don't think I've ever been in a real log cabin until today," Alison said as she wandered around, looking at his things. She picked up a picture of his family. "Is this you?"

Drew nodded. "I'm the oldest of four kids. I grew up here, at least until I was eight. Then my folks moved off the mountain and into town."

"Town?"

"Knoxville. My dad got a job in a glove factory there and my mom worked as a maid in one of the hotels."

"And you became a doctor. That's pretty amazing."

Drew bent down and began to stack logs in the fireplace. "I guess it is. It would have been more difficult coming out of the tiny school system here. In the city, I had a chance to take advanced placement classes in science and that helped me get some scholarship money."

"And you lived here when you were a kid?"

He lit a match and touched it to the paper beneath the wood. It flickered, then caught fire as he straightened. "My father grew up on the mountain. This land has belonged to our family for generations. My great-great-great-grandfather built this cabin with his own two hands. Except for me and Miss Ettie, everyone is gone now."

"How are you related to Miss Ettie?"

She was the most curious person he'd ever met, always asking questions and so interested in the answers. He had a few questions of his own he'd like to ask. Was there a man in her life or was she free to enjoy his company? Did her lips really taste as good as he thought they did, or had he been dreaming? And what did she look like beneath those wet clothes?

Drew cleared his throat, trying to keep his mind on the conversation and not on the shape of her mouth or the curve of her neck. "Ettie's the youngest sister of my great-grandmother, so that would make her my great-great-aunt. My great-grandparents brought her to live with them after her parents died. She grew up a few miles from here."

He motioned her closer to the fire and Alison joined him, holding her muddy palms out to the warmth as she knelt on the rough plank floor. "Look at that," she said, examining her nails. "I'm a mess."

"I'll heat up some water on the stove and get you a basin to wash up in."

"I could use a shower," she said, staring down at her jeans. "And a washing machine."

"No shower," he said, his mind flashing on an image of her stripped naked and wet. "Or washing machine. After I bought the cabin from my parents, I restored it to its original state. Took out the electricity and the modern conveniences. We never had indoor plumbing. There's an outhouse in the back."

What the hell had he been thinking, taking out the plumbing? He'd never planned to have a sexy, muddy woman to deal with.

"No plumbing?" she asked. "How did you take a bath?"

"A big copper tub. I know you're probably not used to roughing it but—" Another image flashed in his brain. A bathtub was even better.

"I grew up living out of a converted school bus. We had a portable toilet, but we were only allowed to use it in emergencies. We showered at the local Y or in a school locker room, anywhere we could."

"Why a bus?"

"My parents were struggling musicians and they played every state fair and flea market in the lower forty-eight. I didn't live in a real house until I was nearly seventeen. Then we settled in Ponder Hill, near Nashville. My mother homeschooled us until then. We had a very unconventional upbringing."

"Interesting," he said. His gaze met hers and he opened his mouth to speak, then snapped it shut, smiling crookedly.

"What?" Alison asked.

"Nothing."

"You were about to say something."

"I was about to apologize for kissing you earlier," he said. "I don't know what made me—"

"No," Alison interrupted. "It was nice. Really nice. I—I enjoyed it." She paused, her gaze dropping to his lips. "And… if you wanted to do it again you could—"

Drew didn't let her finish the invitation. Instead, he slipped his arm around her waist and drew her to him. Her hands fluttered around his face, as if she was afraid to get him dirty. But Drew didn't care about a little mud.

They tumbled down onto the floor, their mouths searching and tasting, and she twisted her fingers through the thick, dark hair at the nape of his neck. A wave of pleasure washed over him and his mind spun with contradictory thoughts. How was this happening? He was kissing a stranger, yet it seemed so perfect, so right.

"If you don't want me to do this, just say so," he said, his mouth finding a spot at the base of her neck.

"No, no," she replied breathlessly.

"No?"

"Yes! Yes, yes. I'm good. I'm fine."

Drew slid his hands beneath her jacket, running his palm from her belly to her hip, reveling in the feel of her skin. He waited for her to stop him, but instead, she arched closer, an invitation for more. And when he moved beneath her sweater and met bare skin, she moaned softly, the heat of his hand seeping into her body.

He slowly drew back and stared down into her eyes. Things were moving awfully fast. And the last thing he wanted to do was rush. "I can't seem to stop myself."

Her eyes were wide. "I know how you feel. It's strange."

Shaking his head, he sat up and crossed his legs in front of him. "Maybe I better get that water heated for your bath. And then I'll make us some dinner." Drew got to his feet. "There are clean clothes in the wicker basket over there. A sweatshirt and sweatpants, if you want to change. And some warm socks."

He levered to his feet and walked away, wincing at the growing erection that pressed at the front of his damp jeans. This was crazy! He'd just met her. And yet, the attraction between them was overwhelming. He'd been too long without a woman in his bed. It was simple physiology. Self-gratification only delayed desire for so long.

But he felt more than simply a physical response to her. He found her intriguing—clever and stubborn and beautiful. And all this without knowing much more than her name and her occupation. Musicologist. What the hell did that mean? It sounded more like a medical specialty than something out of academia.

He had so many questions to ask, but the moment he came within a few feet of her, he didn't want to talk. They had one night together, one night to explore this attraction, and he planned to make it a night worth remembering.

As Drew started a second fire in the woodstove against the opposite wall, Alison slipped out of her wet jacket. Her pulse was still racing from the kiss they'd shared and she could barely catch her breath.

What was she thinking? From the moment he'd first kissed her out in the rain, she'd wanted him to do it again. And now that he had, she wanted more! This was not like her. She was usually so careful when it came to passion. But there was something dangerous about this man, something she couldn't resist.

Her mind wandered back to her conversation with Tess and the little Christmas gift her friend had given her. Maybe she ought to let her naughty side out a little more often. When she was younger, she'd been much more open about her sexual feelings. Was it just a natural part of growing up that sex became more conservative? More…respectable?

She didn't want to be respectable! Alison wanted to be free to enjoy the pleasures that a man's body could give her. She wanted to be so overwhelmed with desire that she couldn't think straight, couldn't control her body or her mind.

Drawing a ragged breath, she kicked off her muddy shoes and socks, then joined Drew at the sink. She washed her fingers in the icy cold water he'd brought in from the pump. When he silently handed her a towel, she dried her hands, then rubbed the towel through her hair.

"I'll give you some privacy," he said as he carried a huge pot to the back door. "You can change, if you like."

The door clicked shut behind him and Alison stared at it for a long moment. It was odd that she didn't feel any reservations about spending the night in this man's cabin. She knew perfectly well where it all might lead and yet she didn't care. She felt drawn to him, to the two very different men he was—the devil and the angel.

He was kind and caring, quietly watching over Ettie, preparing a bath for Alison, helping her navigate down a slippery mountain road. And then there was the man who made her heart pound and her body ache with need. The man who could turn her breathless with just one touch. In all her life, she'd never met a man who was both a good guy and a bad boy.

She found clean sweats in the basket and then walked over to the fireplace and slowly stripped off her dirty clothes. She was cold to the bone and she turned her back to the fire and closed her eyes, letting the heat warm her skin.

Even her underwear was damp. She shrugged out of her bra and skimmed her panties over her hips, then turned to face the fire, hoping to warm the front of her.

Alison felt exhaustion overwhelm her and she stared down into the flames, her thoughts drifting. This had been the strangest day of her life, yet she didn't want it to end. The heady mix of fear and anticipation and desire was like some crazy carnival ride, so…liberating.

She wasn't sure what would happen next, but if it involved kissing and touching Drew Phillips, then she was ready. Men like Drew didn't come along often, especially in her life, and she was going to take full advantage when they did.

Bending over at the waist, she ran her fingers through her hair and wished for a brush. For a long time, she let her thoughts drift to the man who'd rescued her from the rain. He was so…sexy. The way he looked at her, with that lazy smile, and the way he touched her, as if he already knew what would make her writhe with pleasure.

Alison hadn't ever considered herself a sexual creature, although she put great importance on sexual compatibility. But in the past, sex had always come along with a relationship. Right now, though, a single night of toe-curling, mind-numbing sex with no strings attached sounded like the perfect thing.

The door creaked behind her and Alison slowly straightened, her hands still tangled in her damp hair. She glanced over her shoulder to find Drew staring at her, his gaze skimming her body. She fought the impulse to cover herself, curious as to what he'd do if she didn't.

"I—I'm sorry," he murmured, quickly turning to face the opposite direction, the water sloshing out of the pot and dripping onto his boots.

Alison grabbed the sweatshirt and tugged it over her head, then pulled on the pants, smiling to herself. This time the good guy had won out. What would she have done if the bad boy had crossed the room and ravished her? "Sorry," she said. "All done."

Drew faced her again, sending her an apologetic smile. He cleared his throat. "You…you have a beautiful body…speaking purely as a physician."

She laughed softly. "I'll take your word for it."

He crossed the room and stood in front of her. "You don't

have to be afraid. Nothing will happen here that you don't want to happen."

She nodded. "I know. I feel...safe. And much warmer. And if something happens, that's all right."

He reached out and drew her into his arms, rubbing his hands over her back. It was a natural gesture, but once he'd pulled her into his embrace, Alison felt the familiar tug of desire. Their bodies fit so perfectly together and she didn't want him to let go. Drew hooked his thumb beneath her chin, making her gaze meet his.

"This is crazy," he said.

"I know."

"What do you want to do about it?"

Alison sighed softly. "Maybe we should just go with it and see what happens."

"It's a completely physiological reaction, you know. Part instinct, part learned behavior. All of these electrical reactions are happening in our brains and everything feels so good that we can't stop ourselves."

"I'm glad there's a logical explanation for it," she said.

"You're seeing something in me that you desire in a mate. Maybe it's my intelligence or my physical strength or the fact that I can make a nice fire. You don't even realize what it is. You just know that if we mate, I'll be bonded to you. I'll protect you."

"And what are you seeing?"

He grinned. "I'm seeing you're beautiful and I want to enjoy the pleasures of your body. And that's pretty much it for the male side of the equation."

"There has to be more than that," Alison said.

"Well, there is the whole procreation thing. You'll make strong babies. But I'm not really thinking about that right now."

"What are you thinking about right now?" she asked.

"I'm thinking about how you looked in front of the fire,

with your hair all messy and your body so perfect. I'm thinking about how I'd like to take off those clothes and get another
look."

He bent close and kissed her, his tongue tracing along her
lower lip before plunging deep into her mouth. The kiss was
intoxicating, leaving them both breathless, and when he finally
pulled back, she swayed slightly.

"My heart is beating so fast," she murmured. "And my
knees feel like jelly."

"You know how pleasurable intimacy can be and that just
heightens your pleasure when you are kissed."

Alison reached down and took his hand, then placed it
on her breast. "And what will I do if you touch me?" she
asked.

"You'll close your eyes and focus on all the sensations
racing through your body," he said, staring down at her.

She closed her eyes and smiled as his thumb teased at her
nipple though the fabric of the sweatshirt. Though all of his
talk made sex sound like some kind of science experiment,
Alison knew better. This didn't have anything to do with
science. Seduction was an art, and Drew was one very ac-
complished artist.

THE FEEL OF HER FLESH beneath the soft fabric of his sweatshirt caused a current of desire to race through Drew. This
wasn't hypothetical need they were talking about anymore.
This was real and intense.

As he rubbed his thumb across her nipple, a soft sigh escaped her lips and she closed her eyes and tipped her head
back. "I guess we've figured that one out," he murmured. His
hand dropped to her waist, then slipped beneath the sweatshirt. Cupping the soft swell of her breast in his hand, Drew
kissed her again.

But this time, the kiss wasn't tentative. Instead, Drew knew
exactly what she wanted and he was very willing to give it to

her. Sliding his other hand around her waist, he pulled her over to the leather sofa. They tumbled down, their bodies arching together, until she lay stretched out beside him.

"I wonder what might happen if we take our clothes off," she said, her fingers toying at the buttons of his shirt.

He paused, reconsidering the speed at which they'd been moving. They had the whole night. Maybe it was time to take it slower and delay gratification. "Maybe we should hold off getting naked and get to know each other a little better," he suggested.

"But what better way to get to know you than to get naked?" Alison teased.

He groaned softly. She wasn't going to make this easy. Drew grabbed her hand and held it above her head, then rolled on top of her, pinning her body beneath his. "Answer just one question," he murmured, brushing his lips against hers. "Just one."

"All right," Alison said.

He looked at her, meeting her gaze squarely. He'd know if she was lying. He knew all the physiological signs. "Is there a man waiting for you back home?"

Her eyebrow arched. "That's it? That's all you want to know?"

Drew nodded. "If we're going to do this, I want to know that there's no one standing in between us. That we're both free to indulge."

"There's no man," she said. "And there hasn't been for a long time. Thus my…enthusiasm."

He chuckled softly at the look on her face. "Same with me. It's been a while." And now there was a second problem, one that he knew might alter the course of the evening. "I was thinking, rather than rushing into this like two horny rabbits, we might want to take our time?"

Alison frowned. "Horny rabbits?" She sighed softly. "All

right. I understand your point. But if we're already decided, why not just…do it?"

"Well, there's a slight problem."

"A problem?" A frown furrowed her brow. "What kind of problem?"

"I don't have any condoms," he said.

"You're a doctor and you don't have any condoms? How is that possible?"

"It's not like I was planning this," Drew explained. "And I never bring women here, so there's just no need. I do have one in my wallet, but it's been there for a while and it's probably not any good, and as a doctor, I'd never recommend using it, so—"

"I have a box in my bag," she said quickly.

"You carry a box of condoms?"

Alison nodded. "They were a gift." She blinked, a wide grin suffusing her face. "A rather fortunate gift, I'd say."

"All right, then. Nothing to worry about. So, we'll have some dinner, maybe a glass of wine. And then you'll have a bath, and then we'll…proceed."

"What if I can't wait that long?" Alison said. "You saw me naked. I think I should have the same opportunity."

"You want to see me naked? Right now?"

Alison untangled herself from his embrace and crawled off the sofa. "Yes. I think that would only be fair. It would appease my curiosity until after dinner."

Drew laughed. She seemed dead serious. "You want me to take off my clothes right now?"

"They're wet and muddy and you're going to change anyway. I just want to watch. Do you have a problem with that? Are you hiding something under there that you don't want me to see?"

Maybe he was. All this talk was enough to fully arouse him. The minute he took off his pants, the extent of his response to her would be evident. Did he really want Alison to see the effect she had on his body? Or the power she held over him?

"Oh, hell," he muttered. "All right. I'm not a prude. I'm very comfortable with the human body. I just want to warn you about the third nipple. It's—"

"What?" she asked.

He held up his hands. "Kidding. Just kidding. Although it's not uncommon. It's called a supernumerary nipple. About one in twenty people have them. Mostly they just look like birthmarks."

"Take off your clothes," Alison said.

He stood and walked over to the fireplace, then slowly unbuttoned his shirt. As he shrugged out of it and tossed it on the floor, Drew felt a strange shift of power. She was watching him silently, waiting, her breathing shallow.

"This must be how exotic dancers feel," he said softly.

His T-shirt followed, but this time, he threw it at her and the damp cotton hit her face. Alison growled at him and tossed it back, just as he began to unbutton his jeans. Drew decided to extend this part of his show for as long as he could, hoping that his erection might subside in the meantime.

When the zipper reached the bottom, he had no choice but to skim his jeans down over his hips. He stepped out of them, then quickly dispatched his socks as well. Left only in his boxers, he looked over at her. "Any comments?"

Her gaze drifted down to the tent at the front of his boxers. "Nope. Continue."

"You're sure?"

Alison slowly nodded her head. "Yes."

He hooked his thumbs in the waistband of his shorts and slowly tugged. Drew half expected her to stop him, but she didn't. And when he was completely naked, her gaze slowly drifted along the length of his body, then back up to his face. Alison inhaled a long, slow breath and nodded. "Thank you," she said. "You can get dressed now."

"That's it? Thank you? No comments?"

She turned and walked to the kitchen. "Yes. That's all I needed. What are we having for dinner?"

Drew cursed softly. That was her only reaction. Thank you? Had she found something wrong with his appearance? "Soup," he muttered. "Lentil soup."

3

IT WASN'T GOURMET, BUT Alison found that the hearty soup was exactly what she needed to restore her energy and distract her mind. She should have anticipated the effect that Drew's little striptease would have on her and questioned her motives for asking him to do it.

It had begun as a playful challenge, but the sight of him, fully aroused and ready, had shaken her to the core. This was the man who'd share her bed tonight, who'd make her body shudder with pleasure. Everything about him was perfect. Still, she couldn't help but wonder if she was setting herself up for disappointment.

Sex never quite lived up to her expectations. She had always hoped for an experience so intense that it would transcend the simple mechanics between men and women. And she'd never found that, never. Maybe there'd been too many other expectations attached. Maybe if she just focused on this one night and not on the future, she could let herself go.

"What exactly is a musicologist?" Drew asked as he crumbled saltines into his third bowl of soup.

"It's the historical and scientific study of music. I specialize in Appalachian music, or what's usually called traditional American music."

"And what do you do with the songs you find?"

"I write about them, I sometimes publish them. And I sing a lot of the songs in recitals and concerts."

"Are you going to sing Ettie's?"

Alison nodded. "I'm interviewing for a job in Texas. It's a really huge opportunity, but they want someone who can bring the program publicity. It's not enough to just write articles for professional journals anymore. You have to record albums and publish songbooks and perform around the country. And one of the guys I'm up against does all of that."

"So that's why you're interested in Ettie's songs?" he asked. "So you can use them to get this job?"

"Yes," she said. "No, not just that."

He shook his head. "Nobody comes all the way up on this mountain unless they want something. And they usually want it for nothing."

"That's not it at all," Alison said. "If I don't record or publish those songs, they'll be lost forever. Is that what you want? Ettie's name will always be on those songs. A hundred years from now, people will be singing them and saying her name when they do."

"And what if she wants them to stay all hers? What if she doesn't want them to be published?"

"Then that would be her choice. Not yours."

"I'll go get your bath ready," he said. "The water should be hot."

Alison frowned. Maybe she had sounded a little mercenary, but there was a lot riding on these songs. Her whole professional life. She understood his need to protect Ettie's interests, but this wasn't a brooch or a silver ring she was talking about. These were important songs.

She got up and fetched her dulcimer, then opened the case on the table in front of her. She worked out the chords for one of Ettie's songs while she waited. When Alison looked up, she found Drew watching her.

"Sing something for me."

"This is called 'Down In Yon Forest.' It's an old English carol from the Renaissance that was passed from generation to generation. It was brought to these mountains by British settlers. People like your ancestors. They might have sung this carol in this cabin. And shared it with their neighbors." She drew a deep breath and began to pluck an introduction on her dulcimer.

"Down in yon forest there stands a hall,
The bells of Paradise I heard them ring
It's covered all over with purple and pall
And I love my Lord Jesus above anything."

Alison sang the song from beginning to end, all six verses. When she was finished, she drew a final breath and shrugged. "If someone had decided to keep that song to themselves, I could have never sung it for you. Songs are only good if they're passed along."

A slow smile curved his lips. "That was beautiful. You have an incredible voice."

"Not that incredible," she said. "I wasn't really warmed up. And I messed up a little on the third verse." She smoothed her fingers over the dulcimer strings. "I used to dream that my sisters and I would perform together. Layla is a really good mandolin player, but she has horrible stage fright. And Rita hates music, so that was a problem."

"Why didn't you just do it on your own? You're talented enough."

"I'll have to if I get that job in Texas."

"You said your parents sing?"

"Not anymore. I mean, they sing, but just for fun now. My father teaches music in the school system in Ponder Hill, and my mom teaches piano and voice lessons privately. They're settled and happy. I don't think they have any interest in going out on the road again."

He stood, bending close to brush a kiss across her lips. "Sing me another while I finish making up your bath."

Alison sang another favorite, "The Holy Well." By the time she finished a couple more songs, Drew had poured the two huge pots of water into the copper bathtub and cooled them down with another pot of rainwater from the barrel outside.

"It's getting nasty out there," he said. "The rain has turned to sleet."

There was no reason to worry about the weather, Alison mused. She was warm and cozy here and satisfied to spend the night—in his arms and in his bed.

"Your bath is ready," he said, bending over and swirling his hand through the water. "Get in quick or it will turn cold."

Alison crossed to the tub. She ran her hand through the shallow water, then stood. Drew straightened in front of her and she held up her arms, an invitation to him to undress her.

He grabbed the bottom of her sweatshirt and gently tugged it over her head. His gaze slowly took in her naked breasts, then he reached out and cupped his palm beneath the soft flesh of one.

His touch was fleeting. There one moment and gone the next. When he slid his hands beneath the waistband of her sweatpants, Alison held her breath. Slowly, he lowered them down over her hips and then lifted each leg until she was free of them. He held her hand as she stepped into the tub.

The water was only about six inches deep, but Alison sank down and splashed it over her body. Here in this rustic setting, the primitive bath was a luxury. Sleet hissed against the windows of the cabin and the wind clattered through the trees. But she was safe and warm.

"How am I supposed to wash my hair?" she asked.

"Get it wet. I left shampoo on the floor. I'll make up a pitcher of water to rinse."

She leaned forward and dunked her head into the bathwater, then worked shampoo through her hair. But as she tried to rinse most of it out, she got soap in her eyes. "Rinse," she called. A moment later, he was behind her. She held on to the edge of the tub and tipped her head back.

"Farther," he whispered.

A rush of warm water ran through her hair and down her back. Alison smiled as he furrowed his fingers through the wet strands. When he was done, she opened her eyes to find him gone again, but a few seconds later, he was back with another pitcher.

Drew set it down on the floor. "You can use this to rinse off," he said, then draped a towel over the side of the tub. "Let me know if you need me to wash your back."

"Can I ask you something?" Alison murmured.

"Sure."

"Before, when you undressed. I noticed that you were... aroused. Was that because of me? Or was it just that I was a naked woman and you're a man."

"I'm a doctor. I'm used to looking at the human body. I can be controlled when necessary." He laughed softly. "But, I'm having a hard time standing here and acting as if everything is cool. This is like some teenage fantasy come true. It's not because you're just any naked woman. It's you I'm attracted to, not only your body."

Alison stood up in front of him. "Rinse."

He grabbed the pitcher and stood. Carefully, he poured the water over her, smoothing his hands over her slick skin in its wake. It had been so long since a man had touched her that she craved the sensation.

They'd have just one night together, one chance to do what their desire compelled them to do. The water was the perfect temperature and she closed her eyes as he moved lower. Alison took a deep breath and let it out slowly, waiting for him to finish, anticipating what would come next.

When he took her hand and helped her out of the tub, dripping wet, he didn't offer her a towel. Instead, he pulled her against him and kissed her.

HER BODY WAS EVERYTHING he'd imagined it would be, soft curves and silken skin, limbs that moved sinuously and fingers that seemed to touch all the perfect spots on him.

They stumbled over to the kitchen table and Drew lifted her up to sit on the edge, then stripped off his own clothes. The glow from the kerosene lamps cast them in soft light and deep shadow. Slowly, he ran his hands from her shoulders to the tips of her fingers, then back again.

"Where are those condoms we talked about?" he asked.

"In the bottom of my bag." Alison leaned forward and pressed a kiss to his chest. "I think you better get them— fast."

Drew crossed the room and rummaged through her bag. When he couldn't find what he was looking for, he handed it to her. Alison dumped the contents on the table.

"Wow," he said. "That's a lot of stuff."

She grabbed up a small box and held it out to him. "Twelve. I hope that's enough."

Drew laughed. "I think we'll be okay." He set the box beside her, then wrapped his arm around her waist and pulled her against him, her thighs pressing his hips.

"Is this going to happen?" he asked, toying with the damp hair that brushed her shoulder.

"I think it is," Alison replied. She ran her hand down his chest, then paused at his belly.

Drew sucked in a sharp breath as her fingers drifted lower. When they circled his cock, a groan slipped from his throat and he knew there would be no going back. He was hers tonight, and he was determined to convince her that there had to be other nights like this in their future.

"Slow down," he murmured. "We have lots of time."

She drew a ragged breath, letting her fingers drift back up to his chest. Gently, Drew pushed her back onto the table, her naked body laid out in front of him, a feast for his eyes. She smelled of soap and shampoo and he inhaled deeply as his lips trailed over her skin. He pressed a line of kisses along the inside of her thigh, then moved higher, to the spot where her legs met.

He touched her, running his fingers along the damp folds of her desire, slowly caressing her with a gentle but persistent rhythm. She moaned softly and Drew smiled. He knew all the anatomical features of a woman's body, but looking at Alison brought a sense of wonder.

There was so much beauty, so much pleasure to be had, that a guy could lose himself in the need to possess. Instinct drove him forward as he searched for perfection in every kiss, in each caress.

His lips and tongue took the place of his fingers and he slowly drew her closer to the edge and then back again. Her hands gripped the table and at times she cried out in frustration when he'd stop and begin again.

He knew everything that was going on inside her body, every physiological reaction. And yet, he didn't care about that. Drew wanted to know what was in her mind. Did she want him as much as he wanted her? Was this purely animal lust or was there a deeper connection forming between them?

Her fingers twisted in his hair and she sat up, her eyes half-hooded and glazed with desire. "Stop," she said, searching the table for the box of condoms. When she found it, she tore open a package and quickly sheathed him.

She didn't want to wait any longer. She was wet and ready and Drew knew exactly what she was feeling. He wrapped her legs around his waist and pulled her toward him, balancing her on the edge of the table.

Her lips were swollen and her cheeks flushed. Her hair tumbled softly around her face and she smiled lazily. He drew her closer, probing until he found the entrance he sought.

Inch by delicious inch, he moved forward. Alison braced her hands behind her and waited until he was buried deep inside her. Then she smiled and wrapped her arms around his neck, kissing him deeply.

Drew began to move. Exquisite pleasure coursed through his body in waves. Her warmth surrounded him and he tried to recall if sex had ever felt this good. Though he danced at the edge of release, he maintained a quiet control. This would not end until he wanted it to.

Alison buried her face in the curve of his neck, her body meeting every thrust with a soft cry. Drew reached between them and touched her again where their bodies were joined.

"Yes," she murmured. "Oh, that's good."

She tipped her head back, bracing her hands behind her again, her expression tense and focused, her eyes closed. And then, her breath caught in her throat and she was suddenly there, ready to tumble over.

A spasm shook her body. As Drew watched her dissolve into her orgasm, he found his own body ready for release. He grabbed her hips and pulled her close, driving deep before losing control. His mind whirled as his climax overwhelmed him, shudders racking his body and making his knees weak.

When the tremors finally subsided, he collapsed on top of her, his lips pressed to the spot between her breasts. He could feel her heart beating a rapid rhythm as they both gasped for breath. "Sorry," he said. "I didn't mean for this to happen on the kitchen table."

She laughed softly, staring up at the ceiling. "I think I might have a sliver in my butt."

Drew glanced around playfully. "Is there a doctor in the house?"

He pulled her back up, wrapped her legs around his waist and carried her to the bed, the two of them still intimately joined. They tumbled down onto the faded quilt and he kissed her again. "Would you like me to take a look at that for you?"

"No," she said. "Right now, I don't want you to move. Stay exactly where you are."

A SHARP CRACK WOKE DREW from a deep sleep. He sat up and rubbed his eyes, taking a moment to recognize where he was. Alison stirred beside him, her naked body warm against his. The cabin was chilly and the fire had been reduced to embers long ago.

He carefully lifted her arm from around his waist, then swung his legs off the bed and crossed to the hearth. Tossing a few birch logs onto the fire, he watched as the heat from the embers ignited the bark. Before long, flames licked at the wood.

He stared down into the fire, his thoughts consumed by the woman who slept in his bed. They'd made love again before they'd fallen asleep, the second time more slowly and deliberately. He'd had his share of one-night stands in the past, and though they'd served to quench an undeniable need, none of his sexual encounters had ever been as powerful as this one.

Drew cursed softly. There had been a time when he had something to offer a woman—a comfortable life, a nice home in the suburbs, and all the luxuries a doctor's salary could afford. But here, in the mountains, he was living on nothing, working out of an old storefront in a town that was no more than a spot where two roads crossed. All he had to offer was good sex.

But then again, that's all Alison really wanted from him.

Good sex. That, and Ettie's songs. And her dream job in Texas. Why was he so surprised? He'd been focused on his own career to the exclusion of everything else. And when he'd made the decision to move back to the mountains, he'd left behind a disappointed girlfriend or two. There was no difference between Alison and him. They'd both do what it took to find the right situation professionally.

Still, Drew wasn't really sure of her motives when it came to Ettie Lee. Had she slept with him because she'd wanted him? Or was it simply a way to get him on her side with Ettie? He crossed the room and stood by the bed, staring down at her. Maybe she was right. Maybe Ettie's songs did deserve to be sung. But that was his aunt's decision.

Another crack startled him out of his contemplation. Grabbing a flashlight from the mantel, Drew walked over to the door and pulled it open. A blast of cold air hit his skin, causing an involuntary shiver. He shone the light outside, and immediately, it was reflected back at him from the trees. It was as if a million tiny lights twinkled on the bare limbs.

"Ice storm," he murmured. The cracking sounds had come from limbs breaking under the weight of the ice. The front steps were coated, along with the railings on the porch. If the weather stayed cold, there wasn't much chance the ice would melt anytime soon.

Drew closed the cabin door and leaned back against it. Maybe they'd have more than just one night together. Driving would be next to impossible until the ice melted. And there'd be broken branches and downed trees blocking the road off the mountain. She'd have to stay until it was safe to leave.

Drew walked over to the bed and carefully sat down on the edge of the mattress. He reached a hand out to touch her, then pulled it back. When she moved, he held his breath, and when she opened her eyes and looked at him, he wasn't sure what to say.

"You're awake?"

"Something woke me up. And then I heard you moving around. Is everything all right?"

"No."

Alison sat up, brushing her hair from her eyes. "What's wrong?" She drew the covers back and he crawled beneath the quilt and into the warmth that her body created. They lay facing each other, her face visible in the light of the fire.

"Hi," he murmured.

Alison smiled. "Hi, yourself."

"The rain turned to ice. I'm not sure you're going to be able to get home until it melts. I think you may have to stay another night."

"But I can't." She drew a deep breath. "After I talk to Ettie I have to get back. If she gives me permission, I'll have to arrange her songs for the recital and get music to the other instrumentalists. And I have to revise the program and write program notes. I can't stay another night. Tomorrow's Sunday and I have classes to teach on Monday."

"You might not have a choice," Drew said. "I do have a small confession to make."

Alison reached up and raked her hand through her hair, pushing it back from her face. "What?"

"You know when I said the road was washed out? And you couldn't get your car over the gully? I might have exaggerated the problem a bit. There was actually a shallow spot where you probably could have crossed, but…"

"You wanted me to spend the night with you?"

"Yeah."

"And that's it?"

Drew nodded. "That, and now you might be stuck here for an extra day."

She sighed. "Well, I would have had to come back to see Ettie again, anyway." She spoke in a dramatic voice. "And it's such torture sleeping in your bed. I don't know how I'll survive another night."

With a playful growl, he pulled her against him and kissed her, his fingers tangling in her hair as he molded her mouth to his. "Neither do I."

Drew rolled her on top of him, her hips fitting perfectly against his. The friction alone was enough to make him hard again. He knew that they wouldn't stop until they were both completely satisfied. "When you said you had a box of twelve, I never imagined we'd use them all. Now, I'm thinking we might have to ration them."

"I guess so." Sending him a coy smile, she straddled his waist and slowly began an exploration, her lips trailing from the curve of his neck to his chest and lower still. He shifted beneath her, his fingers tangled in her hair.

He knew exactly what she was doing, and though he prepared himself for it, the moment her lips closed around him, Drew thought he might not be able to hold back. His breath caught in his throat and he gritted his teeth, trying to maintain control.

When he attempted to draw her away, she refused to obey. Her only concession was slowing her tempo a bit. It was as if she knew exactly how far she could go before pulling back.

And when she was ready, she smoothed a condom over his shaft. With delicious determination, Alison sank down on top of him. Drew closed his eyes. This was it. This was what he'd been looking for, the perfect melding of two bodies and souls.

Now that he'd found it, how would he ever let it go?

4

THE MORNING SUN GLINTED off the trees, branches drooping and making the woods around the cabin look like a crystal fairyland. Alison walked with Drew alongside the road, their boots crunching on the icy ground as they headed up the mountain to Ettie's cabin. All around them, fallen limbs blocked the road, making it difficult to traverse and impossible to drive. But Miss Ettie's cabin was a short hike and it felt good to be out in the cold, to clear her mind.

She'd woken up that morning, curled into the curve of Drew's naked body, his face nuzzled into the nape of her neck. It had been a new experience for Alison. She'd never had a one-night stand before, but the morning after wasn't nearly as uncomfortable as she'd anticipated.

Once they'd both recovered from yet another powerful encounter, Drew got up and made them a breakfast of granola and canned peaches and coffee. She smiled at the memory of what they'd shared in such a short time. She'd come to this mountain searching for new music, and instead found something—or someone—totally unexpected.

She liked Drew. And maybe after she was done here, she might just make a return visit—or two. After all, it was a perfect situation. They were both completely focused on their work. An occasional weekend together might be exactly what they needed. She glanced over at him and smiled. This was all so strange, so unexpected.

"How long do you think it will take to clear the roads?" she asked.

"If the weather warms, the ice will be gone in a matter of an hour," he replied. "But I don't know if it's going to get warm enough."

"What about your practice?"

"I'll walk down later today and check in. If someone can't get hold of me, they know to call the doctor in Barnwell. I don't have office hours today or tomorrow. I can call about the washout on the road from Ettie's satellite phone."

"Well, I have to leave tomorrow morning at the latest," she said. "If I have to cancel my classes, I will. I am technically working here."

"We'll find a way to get you off this mountain in time for your classes tomorrow, I promise."

Tomorrow, Alison mused. She wasn't really that disappointed. They'd have another night together. Another chance to test the limits of their desire. A shiver of anticipation skittered down her spine as an image of his naked body flashed in her head.

"So what do you usually do on the weekends?"

"I make house calls and do paperwork. Chop wood at the cabin. Run into town and do the grocery shopping."

"You don't have a social life?"

He shook his head. "It's a bit difficult. My patients keep me busy. Sometimes I drive into Knoxville to see friends, maybe catch a movie, but I'm a pretty solitary guy."

"Why did you decide to come back here to practice? There can't be much to do here beyond work."

"I was needed," he said. "I worked at a hospital in Nashville, in the emergency room. I helped a lot of patients, but I barely knew them. I'd patch them up and send them on their way. I know these people and they know me. And I like that."

A memory niggled at her brain. "Which hospital in Nashville?"

"Memorial," he said.

"How long did you work there?"

"For two years. I quit about a year ago."

"I was in that E.R. last Christmas. I tripped over a stuffed sheep in my parents' annual nativity scene and sprained my wrist."

"I didn't treat you, did I?"

"No, I'm sure I would have remembered you. But, just think, we could have known each other back then. But we passed by, not ever…realizing."

"Realizing what?"

"That it could be so…good. Don't you wonder how many other people you walk by that you could get along with? I mean, the stars have to align perfectly to meet the right person. For some people it never happens."

"I guess the stars were aligned this time around," he said.

His words slowly faded in the chilly air, but Alison let them replay in her head. He talked as if this was the beginning of something they'd been waiting for their whole lives. Maybe she had been fated to meet Drew here, on this mountain. But it couldn't be anything more than a casual affair. By the summer, she'd be in Texas getting ready for her new job, not living on some remote mountaintop in a cabin without electricity.

When they reached Ettie's place, the dogs rushed out and greeted them, jumping and whining until Drew and Alison stepped up on the porch.

"Listen," Drew said. "I want to talk to you before we go inside."

"Sure. What is it?"

"If Ettie doesn't want to give you permission to use her

songs, then that's it. I don't want you to pressure her or try to make her change her mind."

Alison opened her mouth to explain she would never do that, but before she could, the cabin door swung open and Ettie welcomed them both inside. The interior had been transformed from the day before, decorated for Christmas. Alison walked over to the hearth and looked at the hand-carved crèche on the timber mantel.

"Oh, it's beautiful," she said.

"I got carried away," Ettie said. "I usually don't decorate unless I know I'll have visitors. I thought you might like to see a few of my things. I've been collecting them for quite some time."

"These are all handmade," Alison said.

"Yes. Some of them are very old. The crèche is something my grandfather carved for me when I was little after I started to lose my sight. I used to run my fingers over the animals and arrange them around the stable."

Alison had only seen pieces like these in folk museums. She could imagine the excitement they'd cause with local antique dealers. But these were Ettie's treasures and they deserved to stay in the family, not get sold to the highest bidder. Alison glanced over at Drew. He was watching her carefully, as if trying to read her reaction.

"I spoke with Drew about your songs," she said. "And I'll understand if you don't want to give me permission to publish them." She paused. "But I think people would like to hear them, Ettie."

"Do you really think so?" the older woman asked.

"I do. And I'd like to sing them."

"Sit, sit," Ettie said. "We have plenty of time to talk about that. Warm yourself. I didn't think you'd come, what with the ice storm. I wasn't sure you'd be able to make it back up the mountain."

"Alison stayed with me last night," Drew explained. "The rain washed out the road just below my place."

Ettie arched her eyebrow, then smiled slyly. "Well, I hope you were a gentleman, Andrew."

"Oh, he was," Alison reassured her. "He was…" She drew a long, slow breath. "Perfect," she added. "A perfect gentleman."

Drew smiled, then they both looked over at Ettie. If Alison didn't know better, she'd swear the older woman could see exactly what was going on in front of her. Her brow furrowed with suspicion and she shook her head. "I've always been of the belief that when something is right, it just is. There's no way to fight it, no way to change it. Just like the sun rising up in the morning, there it is."

Though Ettie's words sounded rather cryptic, they were filled with a simple truth. Alison had met Drew twenty-four hours ago. They barely knew each other. Yet, when he touched her and kissed her and made love to her, her world felt as if it had suddenly come into balance.

"Do you ever worry about Ettie, living up here on the mountain all by herself?"

Drew stirred the pasta boiling on the woodstove, then glanced over his shoulder at Alison. She'd spread out her papers on the table and was humming to herself as she transcribed a song she'd recorded in Ettie's cabin. "She's living her life the way she wants to. I can't fault her for that."

"But she could get hurt."

"She has her satellite phone. I take it down to my office to charge it every so often. She knows how to call for help, not that she will. She's pretty independent."

"I feel kind of bad for her," Alison said.

"She wouldn't like to hear that."

"No, it's not that I pity her. But she's all alone. She doesn't have anyone to share her life, to talk to her at night, to hold her hand when she's sad. I wouldn't want to be old by myself."

"You're alone now," he said. "So am I."

"Yes. But I assume we'll find someone before we're Ettie's age."

"She has a lot of friends. And she was in love, once, a long time ago. He went off to war and died on the beaches at Normandy. And she never forgot him."

"That's so sad," Alison cupped her chin in her hand and looked at him. "Can you imagine feelings so strong they last for almost seventy years?"

"I guess I can," he said. "Isn't that what everyone wants to find? That perfect person to spend a lifetime with?"

"I suppose. But how many people actually do?"

"Not many," he said. "That doesn't stop us from looking."

She went back to work, scribbling her music on staff paper as she hummed. Since he'd moved back to the mountain, Drew had felt occasional bouts of loneliness. But maybe he didn't need a wife. Maybe a lover would be enough.

Alison seemed content here with him, at least in the short term. And maybe that was all he could expect from her. How difficult could it be? She lived in Johnson City, two hours' drive from his clinic. That wasn't far. They could spend the occasional weekend together. Even if she got that job in Texas, they could—

Drew stopped himself short. No. That kind of distance made things difficult. Especially in a relationship that was based on something as simple as no-strings sex. He'd have to accept that what they'd shared this weekend would be all they'd ever have.

He drained the pasta in the sink and poured it into an old ceramic bowl. The sauce was from a jar and enhanced by canned mushrooms and black olives. A bit of cheese on top added the final touch. He set the bowl on the table and then grabbed a bottle of wine from the rack on the counter.

"Dinner is served."

"It smells wonderful," Alison said. "I didn't realize how hungry I was until now. All that hiking up and down the mountain."

"How is your work going?" he asked as he poured some wine into an old glass tumbler.

"Good. I have my two favorite songs transcribed. I'm going to sing them at the recital, I think. They're so pretty and no one has ever heard them before." She took a sip of her wine. "Just think. If I hadn't found that tape, Ettie's songs might have been lost forever. I'm so glad she gave me permission to use them."

"And you never would have come looking for her on the mountain." Drew touched his wineglass to hers. "Here's to happy coincidences."

"I'm glad I came," she said. "You know, if you'd like to come to the recital, you could bring Ettie. I'd love to introduce her and maybe she could give a little talk."

"She won't come," Drew said, shaking his head. "She doesn't leave the mountain anymore. She says when the Lord calls her name, she wants to be right here where she's closer to heaven."

She took a bite of her food. "You leave the mountain, though. You could come."

He nodded. "I'd like to. Maybe I could take you out afterward?"

"There's a reception. But after that."

"And maybe, we could spend a little time doing this," he said, leaning over the table to kiss her.

"Eating spaghetti?" she teased.

"No, kissing." He pressed his lips to a spot beneath her ear. "And touching." His fingers drifted down to toy with the buttons on her shirt. Drew undid one, then kissed her again. "And fooling around."

"Is that a medical term? Fooling around?"

"I believe it's called copulation," he said.

Alison giggled. "That sounds like something you do in math class."

"Not unless you're looking to get expelled."

She stood and set her wineglass on the table, then straddled his lap, her arms around his neck. "If you want to start things up with me, our dinner is going to get cold."

Drew worked at the buttons of her blouse. When it was open to the waist, he pressed his lips to the spot between her breasts. "Spaghetti is always better warmed up," he said.

With a low growl, he shoved back the chair, then stood, wrapping her legs around his waist, his hands supporting her backside. He carried her over to the bed and they tumbled down onto the faded quilt.

Laughing and teasing, they pulled at each other's clothes until they were both naked. Though they'd only been together a short time, he'd learned to read her well. She liked to be touched softly, and his fingertips now traced a path over silken skin.

Drew looked into her face, trying to commit to memory every detail, every perfect feature. "You are beautiful, Alison."

She glanced away. "Not so much."

He reached up, taking her chin and turning her face to meet his gaze. "I'm not sure I want to let you go." He kissed her again, lingering over her mouth. And when he'd satisfied himself with the taste of her tongue, he moved lower to her breast, drawing her nipple to a taut peak.

Was there a way to keep her here for one more day? If he just had another day, he might be able to understand these feelings pulsing through him. Was this simply sexual attraction? A temporary infatuation? Or was it deeper?

She whispered his name and Drew sighed. One thing he did know—this would not be the last time he made love to Alison Cole. He'd make sure of that.

THE WEATHER HAD TURNED overnight, a wind from the south driving the chill from the air and melting the ice. Alison stared out the window of the cabin, gazing up at the blue sky that peeked through the trees.

Drew had driven down the mountain to check on the road. He'd been gone for almost an hour, so she suspected the road had been fixed and she'd be on her way today, back to the real world of students and classes, grades and exams. That world seemed so far away from the one she'd shared with Drew these past couple of days.

Strange that her life had taken such a sudden turn. Over the past few years she'd wondered if she'd ever meet a man who was worth loving. Maybe, at a different time in her life, he could have been that man. But with the job in Texas there wasn't much chance they could continue.

Alison rubbed her arms and walked over to the table, staring down at the manuscript paper that cluttered the surface. She'd crawled out of bed last night, long after Drew had drifted off to sleep, and finished transcribing the melodies of all Ettie's songs.

Christmas was approaching, and after her recital and final exams, she was expected at her parents in Ponder Hill to celebrate the holidays. She'd be a long way from this mountain. She didn't even know what Drew was planning for the holidays. He'd probably drive into Knoxville to see his parents.

She sat down and began to straighten her papers, arranging the pages in order before slipping the songs into her bag. Why was it so difficult to think about leaving? When she'd first decided to share his bed, Alison had accepted the fact that they'd spend one night together and that would be enough.

Maybe it had been a mistake to stay a second night. Maybe

she should have pushed more to get off the mountain and back to her real life. Was that what had altered her perspective? One night was a one-night stand. But two nights—well, that was the beginning of a relationship.

"No," she murmured. "I'm not going to do this." She'd worked far too hard to get where she was to give it all up for a man. And what would she do on this mountain besides drive herself completely crazy? She needed libraries and practice rooms, conferences and lectures. That was who she was.

The sound of Drew's truck startled her out of her thoughts and she hurried to the cabin door and pulled it open. The truth was, she wanted him to tell her that the road was still impassable. She wanted just one more night. But as he jogged up the steps, Alison knew that was not to be.

"The route's all right," he said. "I cleared all the branches and there's a good spot to drive over that gulley. The cold firmed up the road, so you shouldn't get stuck."

It was for the best, Alison mused. She'd get back to her life and forget all about Drew Phillips. "I guess I should get going then."

He nodded, his gaze fixed on hers. "Probably. It's still cold. We might get snow."

Alison retreated inside the cabin and grabbed her jacket, her duffel and her messenger bag. She took one last look around at the rumpled bed, at the fire dancing in the hearth, at the remains of their breakfast on the table, then stepped outside.

They walked silently to his truck, the ground crunching beneath their feet. "I had fun last night," she said. "And this morning."

"Fun?"

"You know what I mean. I enjoyed it."

"It?" he asked, a grin teasing at his lips.

Alison slapped his shoulder. "Stop! I'm just trying to tell

you that…that…it was nice. You were nice. It was amazing. And if you're interested, we could do it again."

"Right here? Or in my truck?"

"No," Alison said. "At a later date."

He pulled open the passenger side door and helped her inside, tucking her belongings between her feet. Drew circled around and got behind the wheel. "That's a possibility," he said. "How would it work?"

"Well, I'd visit you. Or you'd visit me at my place in Johnson City. Or we'd go somewhere for a weekend together. It could be very simple. I don't think either of us wants a complicated relationship."

He started the truck and carefully steered it out to the road. "So we're just talking sex?"

"It wouldn't have to be just sex," she said. "We'd be… friends. Friends with benefits. No strings. Just fun."

"Right," he said, his eyes fixed on the road ahead.

She waited, wondering what there was to consider. Either he wanted to see her again or he didn't. She wasn't going to force him. And it wasn't as if she couldn't get along without him. Yes, the sex was great. And yes, he was the most fascinating man she'd ever met. But she didn't need a man to make her whole.

They pulled to a stop just a few feet behind her car. Drew turned off the ignition, then twisted around to face her. He hooked his thumb under her chin. "Do you really think that would work?"

"We could try."

"And what happens when one of us wants more? When one of us falls in love and the other doesn't?"

"Is that a no?"

He smoothed his hands along her torso, then grabbed her waist and yanked her against him. "No, that's not a no. It's a very interesting proposal. And I'll think about it."

"I offer you no-strings sex and you have to think about it?"

"Maybe I'd like a few strings," he said with a shrug.

Alison studied his expression, trying to read the look in his eyes. Was he really asking for more or was he just teasing? They'd known each other for two days. It was a little soon to start thinking about anything close to a relationship, wasn't it?

"All right," Drew said. "I've thought about it. And I think it's a good idea." He jumped out of the truck, then opened her door and helped her out. "So, I'll come to your recital the weekend after next. And we'll see what develops."

"All right," she said.

"And after that?"

"There's Christmas," Alison said. "Don't you spend that with your family?"

"Yeah, I do. We usually get together at my folks' house in Knoxville. But sometimes we get together at my sister's place in Nashville."

"I'll be in Ponder Hill. So that would be…close."

"All right. See. That wasn't so hard." He reached in his pocket and pulled out his cell phone. "Punch your number in and I'll call you."

"Does this even work up here?" she asked.

"No, but it's a handy place to store phone numbers. I'll call you from the landline at the clinic."

When she was finished, she handed the phone back. "All right. I guess that's it then. We'll talk. Soon."

Drew pulled her into his arms and kissed her. "This isn't the end."

Though she wanted to believe him, she wasn't quite there yet. It could be the end. He could forget to call. And over time, they'd forget what they'd shared. It happened. Feelings faded. Fires burned brightly, then died.

Alison stepped back, out of his embrace. "'Bye, Drew. I'll see you."

He stayed in his spot, next to the truck, watching her as she backed away. "'Bye, Alison. Drive safe."

As she slipped behind the wheel of the Subaru, Alison glanced back at him in the side-view mirror. She put the key in the ignition and, to her surprise, she felt sorry that the car started immediately. There were no excuses anymore. It was time for her to get off this mountain.

She watched him in the mirror, then rolled down her window and waved at him. He held up his hand and waved back, and Alison wondered what was going through his mind. Would they see each other again? Or was this the end of a beautiful fantasy?

5

THE SNOW HAD STARTED shortly after Drew closed up the clinic for the day. At first, it hadn't seemed like a problem, but as he came down out of the higher elevations, it turned to sleet, making the roads a mess.

He glanced at the clock on the dashboard. Alison's recital was scheduled to start at seven. If he found the recital hall without a problem, then he'd have enough time to say hello and give her the bouquet of flowers he'd brought along.

They'd talked a few times on the phone over the past two weeks, but it hadn't been the same. In the real world, they were still relative strangers, without a long list of shared experiences. There had been several silences and topics that didn't seem to lead anywhere, leaving Drew to wonder if what he'd felt for her those two nights in his cabin was an illusion.

To his relief, the campus had signs pointing to the performing arts center. When he reached the building, Drew found a parking spot and pulled in, then jumped out of the car. Inhaling deeply, he raked his hand through his hair and straightened his tie.

They had the whole night in front of them. He'd made arrangements for another doctor to take any emergency calls for the weekend. He'd brought along clothes and condoms for two days and nights. And he could barely keep himself from thinking about what lay ahead—after the recital.

Drew pulled open the front door and walked inside the lobby of the center. It was festooned with Christmas decorations, and swags of greenery and twinkle lights were draped across the wide glass windows. Another sign pointed to the recital hall, and when he got there, a student was standing at the door, handing out programs. "I'm looking for Alison," Drew said.

"Professor Cole?" she asked.

"Yes, Professor Cole," Drew replied. "Do you know where I could find her?"

"She's probably backstage. Through those doors and down the hallway. There are people who can help you."

"Thanks." Drew followed the directions and found himself backstage in a flurry of activity. When he finally saw Alison, she was standing in the midst of a group of students singing harmony to her main tune.

Their gazes met and her eyes registered pleasure. He felt a small measure of relief. The attraction was still there and it was as powerful as ever. When the song was over, she crossed the room and stood in front of him. "You came," she said, throwing her arms around him and giving him a fierce hug.

"I told you I would." He closed his eyes and reveled in the contact. All week he'd thought about touching her, and now that she was in his arms again, he didn't want to let go. Drew held out the flowers. "These are for you."

She looked so beautiful, her hair curled and her eyes smudged with a smoky makeup. She wore a deep blue gown with sparkly things around the low-cut neckline. Drew was almost afraid to touch her, but he rested his hand on her waist and gave her a quick peck on the cheek.

Alison grabbed his hand. "Come with me."

She led him into a small dressing room near the stage, then closed the door behind them. The instant the door shut, she threw her arms around his neck again and kissed him, her lips soft on his. With a moan, Drew dropped the flowers and slipped his arms around her, returning the kiss with the same passion.

It was wonderful to be able to touch her body at will. Though her scent was different, an exotic perfume instead of soap and shampoo, there were so many things familiar to him—the silken feel of her hair, the soft swell of her breasts. When they finally paused for a breath, Drew looked down into her eyes. "I guess absence does make the heart grow fonder."

"I was worried," she said. "I thought things had changed."

"How?"

"I don't know. When we spoke on the phone, everything was so...polite. It was like talking to a stranger. But now that you're here, we're not strangers anymore." Alison stood on her toes and kissed him again. "How long can you stay?"

"All weekend," he said. "I have someone to cover my patients. After the recital, I'm going to take you out to dinner and we'll—"

"My parents are here," Alison said. "They were planning to take me out. But you can come with us—if you want."

"I'd like that," Drew said. "I'd like to meet the people who raised such an amazing woman." He felt a sense of urgency. If he and Alison didn't get to know each other a little better, then the relationship was doomed to fail. And what better way to know her than to meet her parents?

He picked up the bouquet of flowers. "Maybe I should save these and give them to your mom," he said.

Alison laughed as she grabbed the flowers from his hand. "No! They're mine."

Drew yanked her to him and playfully tried to retrieve the bouquet. "But I want her to like me and—" The phone in Drew's pocket buzzed. "Meeting your parents is imp—" It buzzed again. With a quiet curse, he pulled it out and looked at the caller ID. It was the clinic.

"Sorry," he said. "This will just take a second."

"It's all right," Alison said. "You have to answer it."

Drew pushed the green button. "Hi, Sally. What's up?"

"I'm sorry to call, but I knew you'd want me to," she said in a breathless voice. "It's Ettie Lee. You'd better come quick. It's serious."

"How serious?" he asked.

"She refuses to go to the hospital. She says it's her time. It's her heart. Dr. Roy is with her now and he says she doesn't have long."

"I'm on my way," Drew said. He slipped the phone back into his pocket and turned to look at Alison. "I have to go," he said. "It's an emergency and—"

"I thought you said there was another doctor—"

"It's Ettie."

Alison's eyes went wide. "Is she all right?"

"I don't know. She's refusing medical care and won't let them take her to a hospital. If I get there in time, maybe I can convince her to go."

"In time? Is it that serious?"

Drew nodded. "She's eighty-five years old."

"I'll come with you," Alison said, her eyes swimming with tears. "I want to tell her how important she is to—"

"No," Drew replied, holding tight to her arms. "You have a recital to give. And there's nothing you can do. If this is her time, then we have to let her go."

"No!" Alison cried. "You have to help her."

"I made a promise to Ettie and I intend to keep it."

"What kind of doctor are you? You're supposed to save her."

Drew pulled Alison into his arms and gave her a fierce hug. "You need to focus on your music right now. Sing Ettie's songs tonight and tell everyone to say a prayer for her. That's what you can do." He kissed her again, his hands cupping her tear-dampened face. "I have to go. I'll call you later. Good luck."

Drew took one last look at her, then walked out. This was not how he'd wanted the weekend to go. But then, trying to recreate a fantasy had been a foolish notion in the first place. He and Alison spent the majority of their time in the real world. And in the end, the real world might be exactly what pulled them apart.

THE TINY GRAVEYARD WAS set in a small clearing on the mountain. It didn't appear on any maps, nor did it have an address. But everyone in the area had known Miss Ettie and they were all going to her funeral. Alison simply had to ask directions.

Though she hadn't known Ettie that well, she felt they'd shared a special connection through her music. Alison had sung her songs at the recital, had asked for prayers, and yet the phone call from Drew still came. Ettie had passed that night at 9:13 p.m., December eighteenth, before Drew could get back to see her once more.

Drew had called Alison about the funeral and she had offered to sing some of Ettie's favorite songs. Over the phone, his voice had sounded strained and detached, as if planning Ettie's funeral had been too much for him. But he'd gratefully accepted her offer.

Alison walked along the muddy path to the old graveyard, her thoughts on the talented woman who'd lived her life without much notice. She deserved more. People needed to know about her. From her tiny cabin in the mountains, Ettie Lee Harper had carried on the musical traditions of her ancestors. And like a gift, she'd given them to Alison. There had to be some way to pay her back.

A small crowd was huddled outside the weathered picket fence and Drew greeted each guest as he stood beside the preacher. When he saw Alison approach, he whispered something to the man, then walked toward her.

"Hi," he said, leaning close to kiss her cheek. "Thanks for coming."

"I had to be here," Alison said. "For you and for Ettie."

"I think we want to start and finish with a song," he told her. "The service will be short. She didn't want anything fancy."

"I'm sorry, Drew," she said. "I know how much Ettie meant to you."

"She was the reason I came back." He gave her arm a squeeze. "There's a lunch after the burial, at the church. You should come. We can talk." He forced a smile. "We have a lot to talk about."

"Drew, I've been thinking and—"

"No, don't think. Not right now. Can you stay?"

Alison shook her head. "I can't. I have exams to give and office hours. I have to leave right after the service."

After their weekend together on the mountain, it had seemed like such a simple thing to continue seeing each other. But since they'd parted, they had been pulled in opposite directions. Though they only lived a few hours apart, they inhabited different worlds with different priorities. No matter how Alison looked at it, the most they could share was a casual weekend relationship. Drew needed to live close to his patients and she needed to be close to the university.

"I have something for you," he said. "Actually, it's a Christmas present from Miss Ettie." He reached in his jacket pocket and handed her a gift-wrapped box. "You don't have to open it now. Save it for Christmas Eve."

"Thank you," she murmured.

Drew hesitated. "This isn't going to happen, is it?"

"I don't know," Alison said. "It seems so difficult suddenly. I talked to the people from Texas after my recital. I'm their top candidate now."

"That's wonderful." Drew reached up and touched her face. "Do you still want me in your life?"

"Of course I do. But you can't live in my life any more than I can live in yours. How are we supposed to make this work?"

"I'm a doctor. I can get a job anywhere."

"But you belong here with your patients. They need you."

"And I need you."

"Ladies and gentlemen, if we could gather round. We're ready to get started. We'll begin with a song, one of Ettie Lee's favorites."

Alison drew a deep breath and pasted a smile on her face. "I guess that's my cue."

Drew gave her hand a squeeze. "All right. Make it good. Give Ettie a nice send-off."

As Alison began the song, she felt a wave of emotion come over her. Tears pressed at the corners of her eyes, threatening to spill over. But she focused on the music, on the words Ettie had used that day in the cabin.

She was sad for the loss of Ettie's talent and all the beautiful songs she still had to sing. Her thoughts drifted to the story Drew had told her about Ettie Lee's sweetheart, killed in the war all those years ago.

What was she willing to give up to have that kind of love with Drew? The job in Texas? Her teaching career? All of her dreams and aspirations? She stared at the flower-draped coffin. She could never ask him to give up his work here, with these people. What Drew did was life or death. She merely sang songs.

So it would be up to her. If she wanted to love him, then she'd be the one to give up her dreams. Was a chance at love really worth all that? And how often did love fade over time. Alison never wanted to regret her choices.

She looked up and met Drew's gaze. Her heart ached and

a tear escaped and ran down her cold cheek. She did love him, that much she could admit now. But love wasn't always enough.

"WE'RE DOING THE NATIVITY at precisely seven o'clock and not a moment later," Alison's mother called from the kitchen. "And we're all going to be in a festive mood."

Alison sat down on a stool in her parents' kitchen. She'd driven back to Ponder Hill as soon as her exams were finished, packing up the Subaru with gifts she'd purchased and work she planned to do between Christmas and New Year's.

She'd been thinking about her next step. Her interview was scheduled for the first week in January and an offer would be made by the end of the month. But the closer she got to the job in North Texas, the more she wondered if it really was right for her.

"Frank Bellingham announced his retirement at the Christmas party," she said. "There's a tenure spot open at East Tennessee."

"That's wonderful!" her mother said. "I hope they're going to consider you."

"Maybe. They know I'm up for a job at North Texas."

"Texas?"

"Just outside Dallas. It's not far, Mom. And it's a really good job. I'd be starting a brand-new department. I'd have a chance to build it from the ground up. And hire all the best people to teach."

"But you're studying mountain music. Shouldn't you be near the mountains?"

"Yeah, I suppose."

"What's wrong?" her mother asked. "You seem...sad."

Alison shook her head. "I just have a lot on my mind. Thinking about work."

The people from Texas had made their position clear. She'd be the point person for the new department, and with that came much more administrative work than she was used to. Teaching would take a backseat. And her publishing schedule would be accelerated. They expected a book and a recording within the first year.

Alison had been thinking about writing a book on Ettie's life. It would make the perfect summer project. And it would take her back to the mountain—Drew's mountain. The research would be difficult. There probably weren't many people alive who remembered her childhood. But Ettie deserved to be remembered, beyond the simple gravestone that marked her final resting place.

"Your recital was so lovely," her mother said. "I hope they made a recording of it. Did they?"

"Yes. If I go to North Texas, they want me to make a CD."

"That's wonderful!"

"It's just a small, academic label. Nothing big. I'm not going to hit the Billboard Top 100 with the music I sing. But I was thinking that Layla might want to play on it. And you and dad could sing harmonies."

"Oh, I don't know. Your father and I don't sound as good as we used to." Her mother wiped her hands on a towel. "Honey, go see if you can get Rita out of her room. I need her to iron the costumes for the nativity scene."

Her two sisters had arrived home before Alison. Layla had rushed off to do last-minute shopping and Rita was locked in her room, upset about something that she refused to talk about. Alison's father was outside in the cold, trying to prop up the ramshackle stable on their front lawn for just one more year.

The nativity was a Christmas tradition with the Coles and everyone from the neighborhood came. The family dressed up as characters from the Christmas story and gave a concert, which they ended with a beautiful traditional bluegrass arrangement her father had done of "Silent Night." Alison and her parents sang and Layla usually played, although she didn't like it. And Rita, when she bothered to come home for Christmas, stood in the shadows.

"How many Christmases has it been?" Alison asked, reaching for a frosted sugar cookie.

"Ten," her mother said. "This is our tenth nativity scene. It seems like just yesterday I was sewing the costumes."

"When was the last time we were all together," Alison asked. "I can't remember."

"Christmas Eve? It's been a while. Rita wasn't here last Christmas or the one before." Her mother smiled wistfully. "It's nice to have all my girls together again. Honey, I want you to sing those two songs from your recital. The ones by Ettie Lee Harper."

"I will." Alison's thoughts drifted back to the funeral, to the last time she'd spoken with Drew. After the service, they'd stood next to her car, silently holding each other's hands, both of them knowing that this might be the last time they'd touch each other.

She hadn't wanted to leave, but in the end had kissed him and promised to stay in touch. It was an empty promise, but it made saying goodbye a bit easier. Although, it hadn't done much to put thoughts of him out of her head.

She wondered what he was doing, where he was for the holidays. He'd mentioned that he had a sister in Nashville, but for all she knew, he was in Knoxville with his parents. Or maybe even on the mountain, tending to some emergency.

Alison reached for her bag, which was hanging from the back of her stool. She could at least call him and wish him a Merry Christmas. Rummaging through the messenger bag, she came across the small package that Drew had given her at the funeral, still wrapped in red paper and tied with twine. She set it on the counter in front of her.

"A present for me?" her mother asked.

"No," Alison said. "It's a present for me. From a friend."

"Are you going to open it or just sit there and look at it?"

"I—I guess I'll open it." She slipped the twine off the gift and tore away the paper to reveal a digital recorder, much like her own. Alison pressed play and the sound of Ettie's voice filled the room.

"Hello, Alison. This is Ettie Lee Harper. Drew has given me this little recorder and he's told me I must record more of my songs for you. So that's what I've set out to do. Oh, and tell some of my stories, too. But before I begin, I want you to know how glad I am that you and Drew have found each other. He's a fine boy and you could do a lot worse."

Alison switched off the recorder and looked up at her mother. "Who is Drew?" Amanda asked.

"Just a guy I know. Knew," she corrected. "I met him when I met Ettie. He's her great-great-nephew. And a doctor."

"A doctor?"

"Yes, Mom, a doctor. But he doesn't work in a big hospital and he doesn't have a fancy house and car. He works out of a clinic in the mountains a couple hours from Johnson City."

"Sounds like a nice fellow," she said. "Are you...dating?"

Alison shook her head. "No! We're just friends."

The front door slammed and Layla's voice echoed through the house. "Aly! Aly, where are you?"

Alison's mother frowned. "What is she shouting about?"

"Nothing," Alison said. "I'm in the kitchen," she called out.

A few seconds later, Layla appeared in the kitchen door, her hat askew and her color high. "You have a visitor."

"A visitor?"

"Yes! He's standing in the front yard talking to Dad. I walked past and he introduced himself. Tall? Dark? Very handsome? Goes by the name of Drew?"

"He's here? Outside with Dad?" Alison pushed off her stool and threw her arms around her sister, giving her a fierce hug.

"He's here." She stepped back. "Do I look all right? Is my hair combed?"

"You look fine," her mother said. "Go out and say hello. And ask him if he might want to join our nativity scene. We could always use an extra shepherd. I'm sure we have a costume for him up in the attic."

Alison raced through the house and threw open the front door, then bounded down the porch steps. "Drew!" she called.

He turned and looked at her, his eyes lighting up with laughter. "Alison!"

She ran across the lawn and jumped into his arms, wrapping her legs around his waist. "What are you doing here?"

"Right now, I'm helping your dad fix this stable."

She pressed his face between her hands and kissed him hard. "You're the best Christmas present I could have asked for."

"That's good. Because you can't return me."

"How long can you stay?"

"For as long as you'll have me." He set her back on her feet and pulled her toward the porch. "I've made some decisions, Alison. I love my work on the mountain, but I love you, too. I know we haven't known each other very long, but I think we have something very special and I don't want to let it go."

"I don't either," she said, dropping another kiss on his lips.

"So, I figure, I'll move to Johnson City, we'll get a place together, and I'll just make the drive every day to the clinic. And when the weather is bad, I'll spend the night. And when you're off in the summer, we'll go up to the cabin. I've already called and we're going to put in electricity and plumbing."

Alison sighed. "That's all right for the summer. But what happens when I take the job in Texas? I'm pretty sure they're going to offer it to me."

He pulled back. "We'll figure that out when the time comes.

We'll see how we feel and make a decision then. For now, I think we need to give each other a chance to make this work." Drew kissed her. "Just give us a chance."

She looked up into his eyes. She did love him, even though she'd spent the past three weeks denying her feelings. Now that he was here, right in front of her, Alison realized she didn't want to walk away again. If she really wanted to grow old with someone, now was the time to start making it happen. And she knew she'd never find another man who made her feel the way Drew did.

"I like the cabin exactly the way it is," Alison said. "I don't want you to change a thing. And I have some plans of my own, too. I'm thinking about writing a book about Ettie. And I'm going to interview for a tenure position at East Tennessee. I might just decide against Texas. It's so much administrative work there and not enough teaching and—"

"So we're going to make this work, the two of us?"

She stared into his eyes. Alison knew in her heart this was the right choice. She didn't know exactly how it would turn out, but she knew that she and Drew belonged together. Ettie had sensed it, and now, here they were, at the beginning of their own adventure.

"We will," she said.

Drew kissed her, his tongue softly invading her mouth, his fingers furrowing through her tangled hair. This was exactly where she belonged, Alison mused. In his arms. Geography didn't matter.

"Now that you're here, there is one more thing," she said. "We have to find you a shepherd costume that fits. Because you could score major points with my mother if you volunteer for our nativity scene. It's a family tradition. Everyone in town comes."

Her father laughed and they turned to look at him. "I think Drew would make a fine addition to our nativity scene. Can you sing?"

Alison grabbed Drew's hand. "I never asked. Can you sing?"

"I think I'm pretty good," he said.

"All right, then. It's time you met the rest of the family. You're going to get a lot of Cole this Christmas."

* * * * *

COLE FOR CHRISTMAS
Rhonda Nelson

For my mom and sister, who *always* make sure
I have a good Christmas. Love ya'll.

1

WITH ANY LUCK LAYLA COLE would have gained fifty pounds and developed a skin problem, Bryant Bishop thought as he waited on the tarmac for her plane to arrive. He watched Christmas lights glitter in the airport windows, and country superstar—and his boss—Clint Walker's cover of "Jingle Bells" drifted to him through the SUV's speakers.

As Clint's head of security, picking up a replacement mandolin player for the last two dates on a four-month tour didn't exactly fall into Bryant's job description, but for reasons he still hadn't figured out, he'd volunteered to make the airport run.

Clearly he'd gone insane.

In the first place, Layla Cole didn't like him.

In the second place—as if the first wasn't enough—Bryant was too intrigued with her by half, and the idea that she was going to be spending three days with them on the road had given him a sense of anticipation, outright excitement and expectation that he'd never experienced before.

As if Christmas had come early and she was the ultimate present.

Oh, yeah, Bryant thought. *He'd lost it.*

No doubt Layla Cole was going to be someone's Christmas

present—the idea made his gut tense with uncomfortable dread—but she sure as hell wouldn't be his. Long story short, he'd rebuffed her little sister's advances and little sister had evidently cried foul, because the next time he'd seen Layla— another party, another friend—she'd been quite cool. Strange how they kept bumping into each other over the years, Bryant thought. They'd never really traveled in the same circles, but the spheres definitely overlapped enough to be jarring.

Or at least jarring to him. And the great pity in all of this? He thought he'd caught a glimpse of mutual interest in her covert gaze prior to the issue with her little sister. Thought he'd recognized a kindred soul. He'd been drawn to her, had loved merely hearing the sound of her voice, had found himself circling closer and closer to where she stood. Compelled, for lack of a better description.

Which made her all the more dangerous and him all the more stupid.

It was a cocktail for disaster, and the hell of it? He was more than ready to drink up.

COUNTRY MUSIC STARS SURE knew how to travel in style, Layla Cole thought as she settled against the king-size leather recliner on Clint Walker's private jet. She nursed a shot of whiskey—Jack Daniel's, of course—from a cut-glass tumbler and hoped that the alcohol would relax her enough to get her through this first performance.

There was a reason she didn't play in front of a live audience—it terrified her. It always had.

Born into a musical family who'd followed the state fair circuit in a converted school bus for the majority of her formative and teen years, Layla had more experience with live crowds than she'd ever wanted. Contrary to her parents' insistence that she would eventually "get comfortable" with being onstage, she never had. In truth, her stage fright had only gotten worse, and she couldn't have been happier when her family finally settled in Ponder Hill, Tennessee, a sweet little town right outside Nashville with a single caution light and a small square.

Her father had gone to work teaching music at the local high school and her mother had started giving piano lessons. Layla and her sisters Rita and Alison had taken their respective places in public education for the first time in their lives, and while the family still occasionally sang at various festivals, fairs and Fourth of July picnics, their parents had finally surrendered their name-in-neon-lights dreams and bought a house. Her father still kept the bus in prime working order though, and had even built a special garage to house the damned thing. The thought made her smile.

"We'll be landing in five minutes, Ms. Cole," the pilot announced for her benefit.

Nerves attacked her again, making her wince as her belly tightened. She closed her eyes and counted slowly to ten, imagining the twenty wooded acres she'd be able to finish paying off from the proceeds of this venture.

Two performances in front of *thousands* of people, that was all.

She could do it.

She would *make* herself do it.

Honestly, if anyone had told her she'd be flying to Atlanta the week before Christmas to play her mandolin for Clint Walker, who had called her himself to ask for her services, she would have never believed it. But Clint's work ethic and talent were legendary on Music Row and he'd asked with just enough praise and charm to make her momentarily forget why she didn't work onstage. Besides, she'd actually laid the tracks in the studio so it only made sense that he'd ask her to fill in. Then he'd casually mentioned what he was willing to pay her, throwing in a sizable bonus because of the time of year. She'd immediately imagined being able to break ground on her house after Christmas, and any thought of saying no had simply disappeared. She could say goodbye to apartment living.

True, she was terrified to perform in front of an audience. But she wanted her house more, a personal sanctuary, her own little piece of earth. She wanted to plant dogwood trees and wisteria and sip her tea on her front porch while she listened to the little creek burble in the distance. She wanted a cutting garden, herbs and tomatoes, lush ground covers and fruit trees. She wanted an arbor of climbing roses and bird feeders and hanging baskets loaded with blooms dripping from the eaves. And if a cartooned bluebird landed upon her shoulder and she was suddenly hit with the urge to break into song, then so be it. This was her dream, her fantasy, and if it had taken a few liberties with Walt Disney's imagination, well...

Layla smiled and resisted the urge to pull her scrapbook from her carry-on bag. She'd been clipping pages from magazines for years, carefully filling in the white space with her dream home. She winced.

Lamentably, there was no man in any of the pictures at the moment—according to her sisters, she was too picky—but her floor plans called for his-and-her walk-in closets and she'd bought a king-size bed. She was willing to make room in her life for the right guy, but would be lying if she denied her faith in his existence was waning. Layla wanted a guy with an artist's soul and a farmer's attachment to the land, to a home and family.

Tall order.

In fact, she wasn't altogether certain that the artist's soul could inhabit the farmer's body, in which case she might as well settle for one or the other, but was unwilling to do that either.

Picky? No. More like...*particular.*

She'd rather be alone than fill that slot with a man who would ultimately make her miserable. There wasn't much point in putting in all this hard work and planning to build her dream home only to have it turn into the armpit of hell with a guy who didn't fulfill her. Someone who didn't want the same things she did. She'd spent the bulk of her childhood wandering. She wanted to *settle*. She wanted a fancy mailbox with her name on it and a yearly bill from the county courthouse for her property taxes.

She also wanted sex, but didn't see that happening anytime in the near future. It had been more than a year since she'd broken up with her last boyfriend—nicknamed Bitter Disappointment #3—and while she was perfectly willing to consider the idea of a little casual sex, she hadn't met a single guy in the interim who'd inspired her to do so.

Inspiration was important.

She felt the plane jolt as the wheels hit the ground and her fingers tightened around the armrests. Going up never bothered her. Coming down, on the other hand, was a different kettle of fish.

As the plane taxied to a stop, Layla mentally girded her loins for the coming evening and gathered her things. She didn't have much. Just an oversize overnight bag, a tote that housed her small purse and her mandolin, of course. Though she could play almost any stringed instrument, this was the one that owned her. True, you could get a more sustained sound from a guitar or violin, but there was something about the sound *this* particular instrument made that simply spoke to her soul. The mandolin was finicky, required a fast touch and being able to wind its melody through the other instruments gave her a high that no chemical could ever induce.

She loved it.

She took a deep, bracing breath and stepped off the plane.

And it was a good thing she'd just inhaled all that oxygen, because the ability to put air into her lungs promptly vanished when she saw the man standing on the tarmac.

Bryant Bishop. Ultimate inspiration. The inspiration to end all inspiration.

It had been years since she'd seen him. At least two, if not three. But she'd recognize the shape of those shoulders anywhere, and the head that rested upon them wasn't too damned bad either.

He was the *only* man she'd ever dreamed about, and in those dreams, he was alternately rocking above her, gloriously naked, or parked in a chair beside her, rocking on her front porch.

Only an idiot would misinterpret the significance and Layla was no idiot.

Despite the freezing temperatures, her body felt as if it had suddenly landed in the Sahara. There wasn't a molecule inside of her that wasn't keenly aware of him, and her joints—particularly her knees—were undergoing some sort of chemical change that rendered them almost useless. Fire licked through her veins, concentrating in her nipples, and an inferno burned low in her belly. The sensation was so startling that it jolted the breath out of her lungs, making her gasp like a floundering fish. Gallingly, her cheeks blazed right along with the rest of her.

He smiled, almost knowingly, and her mortification was complete.

Bryant had a face that was more interesting than handsome, a series of planes and angles that held character rather than beauty. High cheekbones provided the perfect structure for the lean slope of his face and smooth angle of his jaw. An intriguing cleft bisected his chin and there was something overtly carnal about his mouth. His eyes were the color of smooth butterscotch and held a heavy-lidded quality that gave the illusion of either boredom or sleepiness, whichever he preferred.

Right now he looked bored.

Excellent.

The lightning bolt to her libido and alarming dreams aside, she couldn't say she was overjoyed to see him either. According to her little sister, Rita, he'd once made a play for her and hadn't reacted kindly when she'd rebuffed him. Layla had been disappointed on two counts, the first being that he'd preferred her sister, and the second that he'd behaved like a boor. Honestly, the latter was actually more of a letdown. Rita was pretty. Layla wasn't surprised that he'd liked her. But she'd never taken him for an arrogant ass.

What was he doing here? she wondered. What did he have to do with Clint Walker's operation? Better still, how much time was she going to have to spend with him over the next few days?

Because every second put her that much closer to self-combustion, and the longing that suddenly welled inside of her made her desperately want to turn her dreams into reality.

Particularly the gloriously naked ones.

Desire was a pain in the ass.

2

WELL, HELL, BRYANT THOUGHT as the object of his fascination deplaned and made her way toward him. So much for hoping she'd gained weight and grown scales since the last time he'd seen her.

She was still hot.

He still wanted her.

Damn.

Layla wasn't pretty in the traditional blond-haired, big-boobed 36-24-36 variety, but she had something much more potent and irritatingly less definable. He'd noticed it the first time he'd ever clapped eyes on her—that sensual otherness—and, while he'd managed to put her out of his head for the most part, there were times when her image would simply leap into his mind and rattle his cage all over again.

Bryant didn't associate with women who could rattle his cage, which was why he'd forced himself to steer clear of her. He grimly suspected the woman walking toward him could blow his cage to smithereens if he let her get too close.

After watching his father fall in and out of love with more regularity than a revolving door and witnessing the subsequent euphoria and misery that came along with it, Bryant had sworn he'd never let that happen to him. Love was too mercurial, too unpredictable and, ultimately, too much trouble. He liked his sex straight up with no strings, and any woman who struck an emotional note of any kind was culled posthaste.

Just looking at Layla made his chest tighten uncomfortably, made his skin prickle along the nape of his neck.

In that instant he knew a moment of terrifying inevitability—knew beyond the shadow of a doubt that he would have her before the tour was out and he'd never be the same.

She'd ruin him.

"Layla," he said, inclining his head, because a greeting of some sort was expected and he was nothing if not a gentleman.

Her dark green gaze was amusingly guarded. "Bryant. I didn't realize you worked with Clint's crew."

And from the tone of her voice, she wasn't all that happy about it either.

He smiled, pleased to see that he wasn't the only one uncomfortable. "I'm head of security when he's touring," he explained, taking her bag.

She grunted and he felt her gaze drift over his shoulders, down his back, and settle on his ass.

His grin widened.

"Why do I suspect there's a story in that?" she asked, her mere voice music to his ears. It was husky but sweet. "I don't remember you being in the security field when I met you the first time."

He hadn't been the first time, or the second or third, for that matter. He'd marveled over it before, but it was really bizarre the way they seemed to run into each other from time to time. Friends of friends, but never quite directly linked to any one source, as though they were being cast about in some giant cosmic pinball machine.

"There's a bit of a tale," he told her, a grin twitching on his lips. He stowed her gear in the back of his SUV, then opened the passenger door for her. Looking annoyingly shocked at this display of courtesy, she settled quite primly into the seat.

Layla was petite and curvy with a body more Gibson Girl than *Vogue*. She was small and lush, more soft than athletic and in the possession of an ass that didn't require Apple Bottoms jeans to make a guy want to take a little bite out of it. She had *the* best ass he'd ever seen in person or in print, and just thinking about it made his dick give a little stir.

A tiny smile curled her lips. "Let me guess. There's a barroom brawl involved, isn't there?"

Bryant slipped the gearshift into Drive and made his way toward the exit. "It's not that clichéd," he said. "But almost. Substitute the barroom brawl for a front-row fracas and you're right on the money."

She shot him a look. "Front-row fracas? You were at a concert?"

Smiling, he nodded. "I was. I'm a fan. A guy in the front got a little rowdy, broke a beer bottle against the stage and thought about hurling it at Clint."

"Thought about?"

"That's all he got to do. I stopped him before he could follow through on the action." He shrugged. "Clint was impressed with my efforts and the rest is history. I started out as part of the detail, and when Marshall retired, I took his spot as lead on the touring team."

She nodded, seeming to mull that over. "And what do you do when he's not touring?"

Frankly, given his salary with Clint, he didn't have to *do* anything. He could do whatever he wanted. But that had never been his style. Bryant liked to be busy. Idle hands, the devil's playground and all of that. Even on the bus, he had to have something to do.

While touring he liked to whittle, loved the feel of wood beneath his fingers, watching it take form, then worked on his bigger metal sculptures when he was at home. Nothing gave him more satisfaction than firing up his blowtorch and getting to work, making something beautiful out of old parts and discarded metals. Gratifyingly, he'd sold several pieces and was beginning to make a name for himself. He'd also cast a few personal pieces of jewelry, most notably a pewter tree set he was quite proud of.

"I've got a studio at home and do a little sculpting," he told her.

From the corner of his eye, he watched her expression go from bored disinterest to surprised astonishment. "What?" he asked, chuckling low under his breath. "Is it so hard to believe?"

"Not hard to believe," she said. "Just hard to reconcile. Badass security agent turned sculptor is a bit of a stretch. What's your medium?"

"Metal."

She aahed knowingly and inclined her head. "Not so much of a stretch then."

Badass? Bryant thought, secretly pleased with her assessment, then berated himself. It didn't matter what she thought, dammit. She was off-limits. She was trouble. Layla Cole wasn't someone he could fool around with and walk away unscathed. He'd known that since the first moment he'd wandered into her orbit and had been fighting her emotional gravity ever since.

The monstrous physical attraction only complicated things further.

He could *feel* her, was keenly aware of every breath that traveled in and out of her lungs, every minuscule shift of her body. The scent of her invaded the car and twined around his senses. It was something vaguely floral with warm undertones, reminiscent of lotus petals and sandalwood. It made him want to slide his nose along her shoulder and up her neck, bury his hands in her hair and taste the plum softness of her mouth.

His hands and balls tightened simultaneously, making him shift in his seat.

"Clint didn't elaborate about the schedule when he called. Will we be traveling by bus on to the next location tonight, or will we spend the night in Atlanta?"

"We always build enough time into the schedule for overnight stops. Clint doesn't like to sleep on the bus. We're booked into a hotel downtown this evening, then we'll start making our way down to Fort Lauderdale. A day on the road, then a day to set up. You'll do the final show, then we'll fly home."

"Just in time for Christmas," she said, a wistful note in her voice.

Christmas. Woo-hoo, Bryant thought. Another holiday spent alone. An only child with his father and grandparents gone—who knew where his mother was?—Bryant was officially an orphan. He hated the holidays. Everything closed on Christmas, even Wal-Mart. He'd be eating takeout from a truck stop, parked in front of the television with a nice bottle of wine and his ritual Christmas gift to himself.

On the plus side, he never had to return anything.

Still, there was something quite pathetic about being alone on Christmas, and though he had plenty of friends who pitied him and routinely invited him to their houses for the festivities, Bryant always declined. He didn't want to intrude and he'd rather be home and alone than surrounded by other people and feeling awkwardly out of place.

In the spirit of Charlie Brown, Bryant didn't have a Christmas tree, but a Christmas *branch,* and he roasted chestnuts in his fireplace. It was the one thing his father used to do and was the only "family tradition" he could recall. In honor of that, he'd planted a small grove of chestnut trees on his place and looked forward to harvesting them in a few years.

Bryant had never known his mother. She'd split when he was barely six months old and he hadn't seen or heard from her since. To his knowledge, his father never had either. For reasons he didn't care to examine, he carried a frayed photo of her in his wallet. She was pretty, his mother. Long blond hair, big pansy-blue eyes. She looked like your average girl-next-door, not at all like the type of person who would abandon her child.

But she had.

"Are you looking forward to Christmas?" Layla asked when the silence between them lengthened past comfortable. Her pale buttery-blond hair glowed silver in the dash lights and there was something strangely endearing about the profile of her small, up-turned nose.

Bryant sighed. "Not particularly," he said, effectively ending their conversation.

He only wished he could cut off his awareness of her just as easily. His smile was grim. Short of lopping off his balls, he didn't see that happening.

3

"LAYLA!" CLINT ENTHUSED when he saw her. Tall and lean, Clint was the quintessential country star. He wore Wrangler jeans, a snowy white Stetson and a smile that was genuine. His voice had more character than any other in country music, in Layla's opinion anyway, and she thought he was at his best when accompanied only by guitar. Considering she was here to play the mandolin for him, it would probably be to her advantage to keep that little opinion to herself.

She hugged him. "Clint. It's good to see you."

"You don't know how much I appreciate you stepping in for Rusty."

Oh, she thought she did, if the sizable check she was going to get out of this was any indication.

"Damned appendix," he groused.

She'd known Rusty for years—the mandolin circle was pretty small, after all—and sincerely hoped that he'd be better soon. "How's he doing?"

"Better," Clint told her. "Should be out of the hospital in a few days, but by then the tour will be over. I'm ready to go home, be with my family, but I can't let my fans down, and if we don't play 'Whiskey Dreams' and 'The Long Haul' they're gonna be mighty pissed off."

"Whiskey Dreams" and "The Long Haul" had both been number one hits for Clint this year, so he wasn't exaggerating. She loved that she'd had a part in both recordings, that her sound was there as well.

"You're ready, right?"

She nodded, unwilling to lie aloud. Though she hadn't practiced tonight with the band, she'd practiced all the same. She wasn't worried about missing an intro or hitting the wrong note. She was more concerned with tossing her cookies on-stage in front of everyone. Her gaze slid to Bryant, who was standing a few feet away, scanning the crowd from his vantage point offstage.

His uniform was simple—black boots, black jeans, black T-shirt. He wore several corded bracelets around his wrist and a single cord around his neck. She couldn't make out the charm there, but wanted to get a better look at some point. He'd crossed his arms over his chest, making the muscles in his arms bulge in a mouthwatering display. He rested on the balls of his feet, ready for action, and though she knew he wouldn't hurt her, there was something quite dangerous-looking about him at the moment. He was a predator, looking for prey, and any fool who made the mistake of crossing him would bitterly regret it.

She didn't want to cross him, Layla thought, taking a shallow breath as her nipples beaded behind her bra. She wanted to slip and slide all over him, lick him from one end to the other—all points north, south and in between. She wanted his hot, carnal mouth suckling her breasts, those big, warm hands against her skin. It was a purely visceral reaction, one that she didn't seem to be able to control.

Of all times for her libido to suddenly surge to life, Layla thought with furious despair. This reaction to him wasn't uncommon—he'd always affected her like this, one of the few men who ever had, and his appeal was the most potent by far.

That's what made him dangerous to her.

But now was neither the time nor the place and she unhappily suspected her sister Rita would consider her a traitor were she to form any sort of relationship with Bryant, even the fleeting hot-monkey-sex variety.

She sighed and, as though he'd heard that little exhalation, Bryant turned to look at her. He didn't smile. Nothing in his expression changed. But those melting butterscotch eyes absolutely held her enthralled. She couldn't look away, could scarcely breathe, and the desire that weighted her limbs in that moment should have brought her to her knees.

"So you know your cue," Clint was saying. "You'll need to slide into position as soon as we wrap up 'Lead Me On,' which is second in the lineup."

With effort, she tore her gaze away from Bryant. "Right."

"'The Long Haul' is fourteenth, immediately following 'Right Where I Belong.'"

So songs number three and fourteen. There was a good break in between. What the hell was she supposed to do in the interim?

Clint smiled at her. "We've got an ongoing Super Scrabble game, and so far, Bryant is kicking all of our asses. It'd be nice if you could give him a run for his money."

Bryant? Kicking their ass at Scrabble?

Having heard his name, he turned to face her. The corner of his mouth kicked up into a half grin that set her panties on fire. "You look surprised," he said. "What? You didn't think I could spell?"

"Of course not," she said. "I just didn't know you could win with four-letter words."

Clint's eyes widened, then he guffawed. "I think she's going to give you a run for your money, Bryant."

Bryant stared at her. "I'm up for a challenge."

Fiery chills raced up the backs of her suddenly wobbly

legs. Any more innuendo in that sentence and she'd have an immaculate orgasm, Layla thought.

And if anyone could give her one, it was Bryant Bishop.

"DAMN, SHE'S HOT," GUS Winston said, eyeballing Layla with the kind of prurient interest that made Bryant want to cleave his skull in two. "Not exactly pretty, but sexy as hell." He looked over at Bryant. "Does that make sense?"

"Only if you're writing poetry for her," Bryant told him, tipping a bottle of water into his mouth. He desperately needed to cool off.

"She married?" Gus wanted to know.

"Not that I'm aware of."

Gus grunted, then smiled. "Sweet."

"But you are," he reminded him.

"I know that, dammit," Gus retorted, shooting him a scowl. "I was thinking about you."

Bullshit, but Bryant wasn't going to call him on it. Though the majority of these guys were faithful to their wives, some of them simply couldn't resist the relentless temptation and, sadly, there were too many women in the audience who didn't give a damn if the guys in the band were wearing rings or not. Clint had no less than twenty women a night throw themselves into his path with the express purpose of wanting to polish his knob and he always refused. He was committed to his wife, to his family. He was an admirable man, and nothing Clint had managed to do professionally had impressed Bryant as much as that fact.

Frankly, because of his own proximity to Clint, the band and the roadies, Bryant was propositioned almost as much as they were.

He'd never indulged.

In the first place, any woman who simply wanted to lay a musician wasn't a woman he had any interest in, and secondly, there was something quite degrading about being the runner-up. When he made it with a woman, he wanted to know that she'd wanted him *first,* not that he was just a damned consolation prize when she couldn't land the drummer.

"There's my cue," Gus announced, then strolled onstage. In honor of the holiday season he'd put a big red bow on the brim of his hat.

Bryant hung back, carefully watching Clint and the guys he'd put on the floor. It was nice to be able to monitor from the sidelines, to avoid the crush of the crowd. He tapped his earpiece. "How's it looking down there, Austin?"

"The usual, boss. Screaming girls in skimpy tops, rowdy guys in cowboy hats."

He spied a big redneck in the front row. "Keep an eye on the hoss in the wife-beater, left of center stage. John Deere hat, soul patch. He looks like he's had one too many already."

"I've been watching him," Austin relayed. "He's sippin' from a flask. He could be trouble."

"Keep me posted."

"Will do."

Satisfied that everyone was doing their jobs, Bryant finally allowed himself to glance over at Layla. He'd known exactly where she was—could feel her presence pinging him like sonar—but he'd been trying to avoid looking at her because… Hell, he didn't know. To test himself? To see if he could avoid her?

Because he was an idiot was a better answer.

What he saw made his eyes widen and a hot expletive slip between his lips.

She'd set the mandolin aside, was bent at the waist, taking deep, gulping breaths into her lungs.

Shit.

Not altogether convinced he could help her, Bryant nevertheless couldn't make himself not try. He hurried over. "Layla?"

"What the hell was I thinking?" she gasped, her hands

on her knees. Her voice was thin and shrill. "Have I lost my *freaking* mind? I know my limitations. I know what I am capable of and what I am not, and going out there—" she gasped again, wheezed and choked on more air "—is so far out of my comfort zone I might as well not even have one."

They were halfway through "Lead Me On." It was a four-and-a-half minute track. He had two minutes to get her to pull it together and go onstage.

"Layla, what the hell is the problem? If you knew you couldn't do this, then why did you agree to it?"

She looked up at him as though *he* was the one who'd lost his mind. "For the money, fool! Why else? Do you know what he's paying me? I'd have been an idiot to turn that down! I wanted to pay off my land and start my house. I wanted to plant fruit trees and sweet peas. I'd forgotten about the sweet peas," she said absently, then looked up at him. "Don't you just love those flowers? Aren't they the most beautiful little flowers in the world? Wholesome and sweet. Oh, God," she wailed, her face crumpling. "I can't do this. I—"

He'd often wondered why she was forever in the studio and never touring with a specific band. Mystery solved. "Layla, I don't give a damn about fruit trees and sweet peas," he said, giving her a small shake. "You've got to pull it together. You've got less than a minute and a half to be ready to walk out there and play. Straighten up," he told her, grasping her shoulders.

She resisted. "I can't breathe if I straighten up!"

"Yes, you can." He gave her another little shake and tugged. "Did you tell Clint you'd do this?"

She gave him a wild-eyed, indignant stare. "Of course I did! I'm here, aren't I?"

"Then you have to do it. You gave your word."

Her anguished expression became even more pained and her frantic gaze darted out toward the stage. Her mouth turned white around the edges and for one horrifying instant he was afraid she might actually faint.

His gaze dropped back to her lips.

Clearly a distraction was in order.

"You have the sexiest mouth I've ever seen," he remarked, sliding his thumb over her bottom lip.

She blinked, startled. *"What?"*

"I've wanted to kiss you for years." And because that was the truth and she needed a distraction and he wasn't accustomed to denying himself, he did just that.

He kissed her, and while the earth didn't tilt on its axis, his own world did. Her lips were soft and warm and she tasted like chocolate and mint. He'd expected her to be a bit jarred by his preemptive attack, to be hesitant before fully settling in.

He'd been wrong.

The instant his mouth touched hers, she melted against him like a taper candle too close to a flame. She sighed as though she'd been waiting, too, and then her arms wound around his neck, her hands tunneled into his hair, and she tangled her tongue around his own, sucking it into her mouth.

Layla Cole flat knew how to kiss.

She knew when to slide, knew when to suckle, knew when to lick and knew how to keep the perfect balance of moisture between their mouths.

He could literally eat her up.

His heart kicked into an irregular rhythm, the balls of his feet tingled and a distant ringing sounded in his head—a warning bell he resolutely ignored—as he filled his hands with her ass. She made a little mewling sound and licked a slow path over his bottom lip. Incredibly, he felt that caress along the head of his straining dick and instinctively rocked against her. She was tiny, he realized as his hands slipped over her waist and up her back. He'd never realized how small, how petite she was.

In the dimmest recesses of his mind he registered the final strands of "Lead Me On" and, breathing heavily, wrenched his mouth from hers.

"You'd better go," he said.

Her lids fluttered drunkenly. "Go where?"

He smiled and handed her the mandolin. "Onstage."

She gasped as comprehension dawned, then hurried out.

Well, that had worked brilliantly, Bryant thought, still reeling from the kiss. Maybe she'd need more distraction before her next performance.

One could hope, anyway.

4

LOST IN THE SOUND, LAYLA was milking the final note from her instrument before she had the presence of mind to realize that there were roughly twenty thousand people watching her. She finished with a flourish and waited for the applause to end and the intro for the next song to begin before she disconnected the amp from her mandolin and made her way back offstage.

He'd kissed her.

More significantly, she'd kissed him back.

Quite enthusiastically.

Her cheeks blazed right along with the rest of her and a cold sweat broke out across her brow. Her gaze skittered around backstage until she found Bryant. He was seated at the Scrabble table, arranging his tiles as though everything was right with his world.

Hers felt as if it had been upended and she was hanging on to what was left of her sanity with her fingernails.

"Well done," he said, without looking up. "You wanna play?"

"You kissed me," she said blankly, because she couldn't think of anything else.

He arranged a word on the board, his nimble fingers easily

managing the slippery tiles. He had nice hands. Strong and capable. "You needed a distraction. I was afraid you were going to hyperventilate and pass out."

A distraction? That's all it had been? Despite the instant prick to her ego, she'd almost prefer to think of it that way. Really. If she thought hard enough, she knew she could come up with a reason why that would be so. Why it would be better to believe that he really hadn't wanted to kiss her, but had merely done her a favor.

She was having a hard time being grateful.

"Sit down," he told her. "I'll deal you in."

Because she couldn't think of a single reason not to, Layla did as he directed. He handed her a slide and the required tiles. She quickly examined her letters and then the board. "What did you just play?" she asked, clearing her throat.

This was surreal. Utterly surreal.

"Delicious," he told her, pointing it out for her benefit. He looked at her mouth and absently licked his lips.

Had she been drinking anything, she would have choked. "Definitely not a four-letter word," she muttered, feeling her face flame even more.

He laughed. "You okay, Layla? You're looking a little flushed."

So that's how he wanted to play it, huh? He wanted to kiss her, spell suggestive words on the Scrabble board and then pretend she was the only one who'd been affected. Layla inhaled deeply.

She thought not.

She'd felt a definite bulge against her belly and he sure as hell hadn't had to greedily grab her ass to get her attention. "I'm fine," she said, putting her own word onto the board.

He grunted and his twinkling gaze met hers for the first time over the table. "Lick?"

"Don't forget my double word score."

Smiling, he bit the corner of his lip and jotted down her points. After careful consideration, he quickly played again. *Nuzzle*.

Suppressing a grin of her own, she commended him on the use of his two *z*'s, then set about making her own word. I'll see your *nuzzle* and raise you a *massage*, Layla thought. Gratifyingly, Bryant's eyes narrowed and he shifted covertly in his seat.

"Have you always had stage fright?" he asked. He played a *caress*.

It was her turn to shift. Her nipples tingled and her breasts felt as if they were going to plump right out of her bra. "I have," she admitted. "Made the whole Cole Family Chorus experience quite miserable, I can tell you that. I try to avoid the stage, stick to the studio." She laid *suckle* on the board and waited for his response.

"I can hear you, you know," he said, his lips twitching when he saw it.

She frowned. "Am I shouting?"

"No, I mean, I can hear you in the music. When I'm listening to the radio, I can always tell when you've collaborated, when you've laid the track. You've got a unique sound. It's beautiful. Haunting."

Surprised, she tucked a strand of hair behind her ear and felt her middle warm with pleasure. "There are several mandolin players in Nashville."

"True, but none of them can pull the sound from that instrument the way you do." He played *slow* and leaned back in his chair. She liked the way his muscles moved beneath his shirt, remembered how his firm waist had felt beneath her hands.

"Thank you," she murmured, adding *hot* to the board.

He looked up and his gaze tangled with hers. "Three-letter words?" He tsked. "Are you even trying?"

She grinned and gave a shrug. "I thought I'd stick to our theme."

"In that case—" He quickly arranged his letters, using the *t* in her *hot* to make *wet.* "I'll follow your lead."

Layla felt her nether regions weep and a deep, dark throb built low in her loins. She chuckled softly, then chewed the inside of her cheek. She looked at her tiles and tried to come up with something equally depraved. She settled for *nibble* and imagined doing just that to him. Where would she start? she wondered. Shoulder? Neck? Ass?

"You're up," he said.

She glanced at him. "What?"

"Time to go back onstage."

Panic hit her anew and her palms slickened. She felt her heart accelerate, her breathing go shallow and the tips of her fingers become numb.

He shook his head and sighed, and the sound had as much resignation as anticipation. She wasn't sure what she thought about that, but knew it wasn't entirely flattering. "Clearly I'm going to have to distract you again."

"I'll be fine."

He stood and tipped her chin up with a single finger. His touch sizzled through her. "Better safe than sorry," he murmured.

He kissed her again…and she was neither safe, nor sorry.

Which didn't bode well for the rest of the tour.

Or maybe it did, depending on how one decided to look at it.

"WHERE ARE YOU GOING to plant your dogwoods and sweet peas?"

Layla looked up from the bizarre book she'd been studying—it looked like a scrapbook of some sort—and her confused gaze tangled with his. Bryant slid into the seat across from her. The bus was rapidly closing the distance between themselves and Fort Lauderdale, and though he'd managed to stay away from her for several hours in this confined space, he'd just given up.

Curiosity had gotten the better of him.

"What?"

He sneaked a look at the book she'd been poring over. It was a picture of a two-story farmhouse, clearly cut from a magazine and pasted into place. "Last night when you were freaking out you said you wanted to pay off your land and plant dogwoods and sweet peas. Where?"

She blinked and a furrow emerged between her brows. "Oh. It's uh…" She smiled, a bit self-consciously, and tucked her hand behind her neck. "It's just a little piece of property close enough to my parents to make them happy, but far enough to keep me sane."

He chuckled. "Sounds like a good plan. They're in Ponder Hill, right?"

She looked surprised that he remembered, her green eyes widening prettily. Pathetic how he'd filed every little nugget of information about her away in his mind, unwilling to forget a single detail. Furthermore, though he didn't live in Ponder Hill proper, he still held the same address.

"Yeah," she said. "I'm about ten miles from them, out in the country."

"Really?" He was, too. A strange tingling had started low in his back.

"How much land?" he asked casually.

"Twenty acres out on Hardscrabble Road," she told him, her lips twisting with wry humor. "It wasn't the picturesque address I'd imagined, but the property is beautiful. Lots of hardwoods and a nice building spot."

He felt a smile slide slowly across his lips. "Met your neighbors yet?"

Unbeknownst to her, she was sitting across the table from one. He'd wondered who'd bought that property, but had never gone to the trouble to find out. He had plenty of room on his own twenty-acre farm and had built so far back into the plot that his house wasn't visible from the road.

"No," she said. "I didn't see the point until I actually moved out there."

To tell her or not to tell her, that was the question. For whatever reason…he decided not to. He'd let that be a little surprise.

"When do you break ground?"

"I promised myself that I wouldn't start the house until the land was paid for—I wanted to completely own that little part of the earth first, you know?" She shook her head, looked away as though confessing something she regretted. "It probably doesn't make sense, but—"

"No, it makes perfect sense." He smiled. "And the bank typically likes that plan as well."

She grinned and peered up at him from lowered lashes. "True." She sighed. "Anyway, looks like I'll be breaking ground after the first of the year."

His knee bumped hers beneath the table and that lone contact made him react. "Miserable time to get started. The weather's terrible."

"I want to be in by spring," she said. "I want to start planting."

He inspected a single charm attached to his bracelet. He'd cast it himself. It was a tree, complete with roots. He knew exactly where she was coming from on this. His father had been a perpetual renter, had never owned anything more than the cars that took them from place to place. He inclined his head knowingly. "Ah, yes. The dogwoods and sweet peas."

She nodded primly. "And lots of other stuff, too. But those are my favorites. I'm looking forward the most to watching them grow."

"Any particular significance?"

She seemed to mull that over. "The dogwoods I just love. Hearty little trees, delicate flowers. They're beautiful." Her gaze turned inward and she lifted a shoulder. "My grandmother always had sweet peas. She'd set little bouquets of them in every room, put them in Mason jars. They were simple but pretty, and I love the scent."

Good enough reason, Bryant thought. He'd never gotten to know his grandparents. His father's parents had died before he was born, and his mother's parents... Well, he didn't have any idea where they were or if they even knew about him. He'd often toyed with the idea of trying to track them down—not his mother, because she definitely knew about him and hadn't wanted him. But with his grandparents there was always the possibility that they hadn't known. Maybe that would be his Christmas present to himself this year, Bryant thought. Maybe he'd try to fill in a few blanks on his family tree.

He was never more aware of being alone than this time of year. When other people talked about Christmas presents, baked ham and Aunt Rose's terrible fruit cake, he got an uncomfortable knot in his belly because he never had anything to add. Take now, for instance. Trick, the sound guy, was currently in a bidding war with someone on eBay for some sort of fake hamster that ran on batteries, and Mason Carpenter, lead guitarist, was wrapping presents for his girls. Chuck Murray, a fellow security agent, had been bemoaning the hectic Christmas schedule and how he'd like a simple holiday at home without playing musical houses.

He should be grateful he had somewhere to go, in Bryant's opinion.

"I guess I should thank you," she said somewhat shyly. She slid her fingers over the corners of her book. He remembered the small calluses on her fingertips against his skin and his blood heated. She felt right. She tasted right. She fit, for lack of a better description. And she was his neighbor. Coincidence? Bryant wondered. Or fate?

He smiled. "Thank me for what?"

"For distracting me. I wouldn't have been able to have gone on without your—" She struggled to find the right word.

"Tongue?" he supplied helpfully.

She blushed, chuckled low under her breath. "I was going to say 'assistance,' but tongue works just as well, I suppose."

"It was my pleasure." Truer words had never been spoken.

"It definitely did the trick."

He leaned back and laced his hands behind his head. "Especially considering you don't like me, huh?"

Her gaze flew to his and the grin turned a bit guilty. "Who said I didn't like you?"

"Who had to?"

"I like you well enough," she told him. She grimaced. "But my sister doesn't."

There we go. The heart of it. He knew this conversation was inevitable and it was better to get it over with before he slept with her. He'd given up any pretense of pretending, even to himself, that sex wasn't going to happen between them.

It was.

It was as inevitable as this damned conversation he didn't want to have.

Yet they had to have it. He wanted her. He ached for her. He needed her…and Bryant Bishop wasn't used to *needing* anyone. Layla Cole was like a virus under his skin and the resulting fever was burning him up. Bedding her was the cure, he knew, and even if it wasn't, then at least he'd have had her. At least he would have buried himself into her heat, felt her sweet little body wrapping around his.

And that, he told himself, would be enough.

Whatever it was that was making her—and had always

made her—so irresistible would wane after he'd bedded her and the mystique was gone. Right? Right.

He liked this plan and had every intention of putting it into play tonight when they settled in at the hotel. Bryant grinned.

He'd give her a distraction she'd never forget.

5

HE WINCED. "I'M NOT surprised your sister doesn't like me," Bryant readily confessed, to Layla's immense shock.

She sagged like a spent party balloon and mentally swore. She'd been secretly hoping that he'd either play dumb or deny it so they could continue to play dirty Scrabble like they had last night, and he could keep using his kiss therapy to keep her stage fright at bay. She'd actually done better onstage than she'd expected and she didn't know how much of that was thanks to Bryant.

"Women don't like being thwarted any more than men do," he continued with a casual shrug, "and I'm sure that when I told her I wasn't interested I became one of her least favorite people." Half of his mouth lifted into a wry smile. "I got the impression she's not used to being told no."

Layla blinked, confused. "I'm sorry, what? What do you mean she's not used to being told no?"

He shrugged. "She hit on me." His gaze tangled significantly with hers. "I wasn't interested. Another Cole girl had already caught my eye."

"*She* hit on *you?*" she repeated, still reeling from his version of what happened. Much as she loved Rita, in retrospect Bryant's version made more sense.

He lifted one shoulder in a negligent shrug. "She'd had too much to drink," he said. "It happens." He grinned again. "But probably not to you. I get the impression that you like to be in control."

He'd pegged her right. Honestly, Layla liked a fruity cocktail as much as the next person but didn't have any desire to get drunk. She never had. She didn't like feeling out of control or nauseated or any of the side effects that came along with having too much to drink. She liked to get a buzz every once in a while, just enough to make her laugh a little too loudly, but otherwise that was the extent of her recreational drug use. She shared as much with Bryant.

"Judging from your reaction, I take it your sister gave you a different version of events."

She nodded. "Rita said it was you that wouldn't take no for an answer."

He merely grinned. "Not to sound arrogant, Layla, but there are too many women who say yes for me to worry about one saying no."

Didn't she know it? Layla thought, her belly going all hot and muddled from watching his mouth. It was overtly carnal. And she loved the way it had felt against her own.

She wasn't going to touch that comment with a ten-foot pole. "Rita has calmed down a bit," she said instead. "She's still looking for Mr. Right though."

"What about you?" he asked, studying her from beneath a sweep of lashes that would make a supermodel envious. "Is Mr. Right going to help you build your house?"

He was fishing, Layla realized, and resisted the urge to preen. "No," she admitted. "But I'm willing to accept all of the help I can get, so that would include Mr. Right, Mr. Wrong, Mr. Right Now and Mr. Maybe." She laughed. "I can hook every one of them up with a hammer."

His laugh echoed between them, warm and strangely soothing. "Any able-bodied man then?"

She took a sip of her soda. "That's about the size of it, yes."

He shot her a speculative look. "Maybe I'll give you a hand."

A bubble of anticipation rose to the top of her belly and popped. "You know your way around a nail gun?"

His gaze met hers and something wicked lingered there, making the tops of her thighs catch fire. "I'm good with my hands."

Oy. She'd just bet he was.

He leaned forward. "Can I be straight with you, Layla?"

What was she supposed to say to that? No, please lie? She was absolutely certain this conversation was about to take a turn that was going to lead her straight into his bed.

As if she hadn't been destined to wind up there at some point or another since the second she'd laid eyes on him. She'd been carrying a sexual torch for him that had made every flicker or flame she'd felt for other men pale in comparison.

She swallowed, nodded. "Sure," she said, hoping she sounded offhand. "Go ahead."

He leaned forward, his gaze intense. "Something about you just trips my trigger, you know? Just sets me off. I feel you even when I'm not touching you and when I do touch you…" His gaze skimmed over her face, settled hotly on her mouth. "It's like sexual crack. Tomorrow night after the show, we're both going to go our separate ways, but I was really hoping that you'd spend a little time with me tonight."

Wow. She'd never had a guy lay it on the line quite so…explicitly. Without the let's-go-to-dinner-and-see-what-happens dance. In a nutshell, he wanted her and was willing to tell her that without the so-called traditional dating prelude. It was exhilarating. Refreshing. Disconcerting, too, if she were honest.

"I don't need distracting tonight, Bryant."

A wicked smile crossed his lips. "You might not need it, but I can make you want it."

Blood boiled beneath her skin at the blatant sexual bravado in that simple sentence. Her hoo-hah caught fire and she resisted the urge to make sure that steam wasn't seeping out of her panties.

"What do you say, Layla? You up for a little mutual enjoyment?"

Mutual enjoyment with a guy who'd likened her to sexual crack? Oh, yeah. She was up for that. Because it was him. Because, against all reason, something about him made her feel…safe.

And he hadn't played her. A girl always knew where she stood with Bryant Bishop.

Or maybe where she *lay* was a better analogy.

JUST BECAUSE HE'D BASICALLY alerted Layla to his sexual intention didn't mean that he didn't know how to treat a lady. While his father hadn't been very good at keeping a woman around, he'd been stellar at attracting them in the first place. This meant being courteous—opening doors, pulling back chairs, a light touch at the small of her back.

Though he could have said something like he wanted to feed her because she was going to need her strength later in the evening, Bryant kept dinner conversation on an even keel and devoid of much sexual innuendo. The hotel restaurant was decked out in its Christmas finery with lots of tinsel and candlelight, and the waitresses all wore flashing pins that read "Ho Ho Ho."

The truth was, he simply enjoyed Layla's company. More than was strictly advisable, if he were honest with himself.

He liked listening to the sound of her voice—a strange combination of husky and smooth—watching the way her eyes moved. Sweeping glances, lowered lashes, a twinkling.

Every emotion was telegraphed by those amazingly expressive eyes.

Her hair was equally vibrant. Long, loose, buttery curls framed her elfin face, trailed over her small shoulders and settled just above the back of her bra. She had the most amazing complexion, too. Creamy, like a porcelain doll, with an underlying wash of pink. Her upper lip was slightly off center, adding enough imperfection to make her interesting. For reasons he couldn't explain, there was something fundamentally sexy about that flaw.

She smiled self-consciously. "You're staring."

"You're beautiful."

Her eyes glittered and a becoming rose spread over her cheeks. "That's not necessary, you know. You had me at 'sexual crack.'"

He shook his head. "It's the damnedest thing, Layla. I've been jonesing for you since the first time I saw you. If I hadn't dawdled in making my move at Jeb's party, your sister would have never hit on me—or at least, I hope not—and I would have made a play for you then."

She studied him thoughtfully. "What about a couple of years ago, at Chris and Maggie's New Year's Eve party? What stopped you then?"

He laughed. "That death ray glare you gave me."

Her mouth gaped. "I didn't give you a death ray glare."

"Bullshit. My skin should have melted off." He tipped his longneck up. "You'd already decided you didn't like me by then."

"Maybe," she admitted. "But it didn't keep me from thinking you were hot."

Masculine pride made his chest puff and he felt his lips twitch with pleasure. "Ah. So you liked it when I distracted you?"

"It could easily become one of my favorite pastimes."

Bryant had been in a state of semi-arousal since they'd

entered the hotel restaurant, but with that little admission he went painfully hard.

She wanted him.

She gazed at his chest and quirked a brow. "I like that pendent," she told him. "It caught my eye yesterday, but I was too stressed over my impending performance to comment on it. It's a tree, right? Like the one on your bracelet."

"It is, thanks."

She reached across the table and inspected the little charm, her cool fingers brushing against his too-warm skin. The merest touch of her fingers made something in his chest flutter and expand. "It's lovely. Silver?"

"Pewter," he corrected. He swallowed. "I cast it myself."

Her eyes widened with obvious delight. "Seriously?"

"Seriously."

"Wow. That's cool. Do you do a lot of this?"

"Only when the mood strikes."

Her forehead wrinkled in concentration. "It's so detailed. You're very good. Just men's jewelry then?"

"For the most part," he told her. "I don't use a lot of stones— prefer to work with metal." He grinned. "Women tend to like more sparkly things."

"I like amethysts," she said, pointing to the pendent around her neck.

He'd noticed. "That's nice. Where'd you get it?"

"Sedona."

Bryant inclined his head. "Vacation?"

She nodded. "Yeah. It's lovely. And the energy is just… amazing."

"So I've heard."

"You've never been?" she asked.

"Driven through on the way to somewhere else, but didn't stop." He grinned. "I don't suppose that counts?"

She shook her head. "Sorry, no. You should go sometime. You'd like it. Lots of artists there. You'd fit right in."

He cocked his head. "You trying to run me out of Davidson County?"

"You're still there?" she asked.

He nodded, unwilling to elaborate on exactly where he lived. Why not? Who knew? But he hung on to that little tidbit all the same.

She hesitated and he felt the impending shift in the conversation. "My sister isn't going to appreciate this," she said, and he interpreted *this* to be the fabulous sex they were about to have.

He covered the check with a sizable bill, took her hand and pulled her from the booth. "Then I guess it's a good thing she isn't here."

Time to get her out of his system once and for all, Bryant thought. If Layla was the disease, then sex was the cure.

It had to be…because anything else was unthinkable.

6

IN THE PART OF HER BRAIN that wasn't consumed with getting naked with Bryant, Layla realized that this part-time security agent/jewelry maker/metal sculptor who was wearing a pendent of a tree was the closest thing to an artist's soul with a farmer's body she was ever going to get.

And he had "temporary" tattooed all over him. He'd even alluded to the fact that they would go their separate ways tomorrow night after the final concert, that they wouldn't see each other again.

She knew this, and yet part of her hoped for something more. Part of her knew that Bryant Bishop was the yin to her yang, the peg for her hole (no sexual pun intended), the refrain for her melody. She knew it, but would not dwell on it.

At least not tonight.

His fingers threaded through hers, Bryant casually led her out of the restaurant to the lobby, where he depressed the call button for the elevators.

"Dinner was wonderful. Tha—"

The doors closed behind them and he ate what was left of her thank-you. His mouth unerringly found hers with an urgency and desperation she hadn't expected but felt all the same. His tongue tangled expertly around hers and she could feel the long, hard length of him nudging determinedly against her belly.

Her mouth watered.

She tugged his shirt from the waistband of his jeans and found the warm skin at the small of his back. He shuddered and deepened the kiss, and she felt the smooth suction of his mouth against hers down low in her belly. His hands slipped over her back, then beneath her shirt, and the first touch of his fingers against her bare skin snatched the breath from her lungs. A shaky laugh rattled up her throat.

Oh, this was going to be good.

"I'm amusing you?" he asked between kisses. "Clearly I'm not trying hard enough."

She snickered again. "Oh, I don't know about that. It *feels* hard enough."

It was his turn to laugh and she felt that rumble against her chest as he lifted her up. She wrapped her legs around his waist and he cradled her ass, then gave a gentle squeeze. Her sex wept and a low, insistent throb quickened in her clit, sharing the same beat as her heart.

The elevator doors slid open and he hurried down the hall with her clinging to him. Without dropping her or breaking the kiss, he managed to get his hotel room door open.

Neat trick, that.

Five seconds later she was flat on her back on the bed and he was between her legs, flexing against her while they were still fully clothed. He was heavy and hard and...*damn*.

"This...would be...so much...better...naked," she gasped, her hands tearing his shirt over his head. Smooth skin, sleek muscle, no man-scaping. Any guy who worried more about excess body hair than she did made her nervous. There were tiny scars on his chest—burns from bits of metal, she realized, leaning forward to lick one.

He shuddered above her.

The power was heady and she knew the smile that rolled across her lips was wicked.

"I don't trust that grin," he said, those keen butterscotch eyes missing nothing.

"Smart boy."

"Boy?" he said, feigning outrage. "I beg to differ."

She reached down and tugged at his zipper. "I'd like for you to beg."

He chuckled, baring her midriff so that he could kiss his way up her middle. "I'd like for *you* to beg."

She was on the verge of making a boner reference when he popped the front clasp on her bra and took the beaded crest of her breast fully into his mouth. His tongue laved her nipple, abrading it in the most delicious way. He suckled her and she felt that tug deep in the heart of her sex, as though there were a corresponding thread connecting the two. A broken gasp sounded between them—hers—and she squirmed against him, needing to feel the hardest part of him against the softest part of her.

She settled for slipping her hand beneath his boxers and palming him. His penis jumped into her greedy hand like a happy puppy waiting to be petted, and she encircled him and began to stroke.

He retaliated by thumbing her other nipple, then licked a path between the two and feasted on the previously neglected one. The small of her back left the bed and she shifted her hips, a soundless entreaty that he answered by stripping the rest of her clothes off, leaving her bare and open to his hungry gaze.

"You're beautiful," he said.

She never enjoyed compliments about her body. They made her feel self-conscious and weird. "I'm a sure thing," she told him. "No flattery necessary."

"Stop that," he said. "You—" he kissed a rib "—are—" he slid his nose down to her belly button "—beautiful." He drew back, retrieved a condom from his wallet, then quickly rolled it into place. A second later he was nudging the pouting folds of her sex, bumping her clit in the process.

"You're pretty damned gorgeous yourself," she said, meaning every word. He was glorious, utterly perfect, and for this moment, hers. "Come inside me," she said, rocking against him.

Then he filled her up and she stopped thinking altogether. She could only feel…and it was heavenly.

Ultimate inspiration indeed.

Come inside me.

Bryant hesitated for a fraction of a second—was sure she didn't notice—before he took the literal plunge into her body. A last-ditch effort at self-preservation, he realized.

But too late.

One second he was Bryant Bishop, completely and totally in control of his future. The next, he was inside her and he was no more the master of his fate than the man in the moon.

He was lost.

Sensation bombarded him on all sides, and while the rest of his body felt as though it was free-falling, he had the most peculiar awareness deep down in his chest of being rooted— of belonging. Had she not bent forward and licked his nipple at that moment, he would have lingered on the feeling, then panicked.

But she did and he dove deeper, determined to fix whatever was wrong with him. If he took her hard enough, fast enough, he could make things right again. He could change whatever had just happened to him.

Her greedy feminine muscles clamped around him, holding him as he plunged in and out of her. Her breasts were full and lush, capped with pale pink rosy nipples, and watching her flat belly undulate beneath his, the line of her hips shift up to meet his, was quite possibly the most erotic thing he'd ever done.

She smoothed her hands over his chest, along his shoulders, then around his neck, and drew him down to kiss her once more. The combination of tasting her while he took her was somehow more rewarding—more significant—than it had ever been. She drew her legs back, allowing him more access, and wrapped them around his waist until the bottoms of her feet rested against his ass. He shut his eyes to keep them from rolling back in his head.

"Woman, you are killing me," he growled against her mouth.

"Good," she said, upping the tempo between them. "I'm sure you deserve it for something."

He chuckled, surprised at her insight, particularly at the moment. "I'm sure you're right."

"I usually am."

"And so modest, too."

She laughed and he felt the vibration around his dick. The sensation kindled that first flash of beginning orgasm and he pounded harder. Sensing the change, Layla met his pace thrust for thrust. She licked his neck, nibbled at his shoulders and slid her hands over his back. She was everywhere, beneath his body and beneath his skin, and the scent of her curled around his senses, drugging him.

He heard her breath catch and her own rhythm increased, her muscles fisting more and more tightly around him. He slipped his arm beneath her back, angling her up and more tightly against him. The new position made his balls slap against her and he nailed her clit with every thrust, which had been the intent after all. He knew his way around a woman's body and that little nub hidden at the top of her sex was the money spot. He knew he could pound, twist, aim and angle all night in her velvety channel, but if he didn't pay homage to that little part of her anatomy, it was all in vain. Just like that strip of flesh at the base of his balls did it for him—which she was currently stroking, the she-devil—this was her hot button.

Her mouth opened and a slow smile gratifyingly curled the edges and he knew that she was close. Thank God, because so was he.

He pounded harder, in and out, in and out, and felt her slide across the slippery bedspread with every brutal thrust into her body. Any minute now they were in danger of falling completely off the bed. Her breathing came in rapid little puffs, ragged and uneven, and a groan rumbled low in her throat. He knew that sound, knew what it meant, and worked harder. He bent his head, drew her breast into his mouth and sucked deeply.

She bucked hard once, twice, then every muscle in her body locked down tight as those around him contracted over and over again.

Her release triggered his own and the orgasm shot from his loins like a bullet down the barrel of a gun. He dug his toes into the mattress and nudged deep, seating himself firmly inside her. Nothing short of the Jaws of Life could have gotten him out of there at the moment, Bryant thought dimly as his vision blackened around the edges and a bone-deep shiver eddied up his spine. Contentment washed through him, raising every hair on his body, and he sagged against her, utterly spent and completely sated. He kissed her neck, then taking her with him, rolled to the side. He made quick work of removing the condom, then settled her more securely into the crook of his arm.

She fit.

And he was doomed.

"Fair warning," Layla said, and he could hear the smile in her voice. "I'm gonna wanna do some more of that."

Whatever he'd expected her to say, it hadn't been that, and her frankness startled a laugh right out of him. He doodled on her upper arm, enjoyed the feel of her naked breast against his chest.

"The tour's over tomorrow night," he said. A warning, but one he felt he needed to make. He was temporary. This was temporary. He didn't do committed or permanent. It wasn't in the genes.

She was different and he felt differently about her. He'd even go so far as to say that she was special. But that didn't change anything.

And until this moment, he'd always been fine with that.

Something told him he wasn't going to be fine anymore.

7

WARNING HER, WAS HE? As if she'd expected anything more than a brief but beautiful thing between them. Any woman with a grain of sense knew that Bryant Bishop wasn't the kind of guy who would be easily domesticated. Did her heart give a little pang at this knowledge?

Definitely.

She felt a strange sort of connection to him, a sense of hope and rightness she'd never experienced before.

But she wasn't stupid, and letting her heart get tangled up in the strings of the best sex she'd ever had was the height of idiocy.

She wouldn't allow herself to do that. She was going to enjoy him. That was all. She snuggled in closer and nuzzled his neck with her nose.

"I love the way you smell," she said. "It's like musk and wood. Resinous." She waited a beat. "Sort of like a Christmas tree."

She felt his silent laugh vibrate against her cheek. "A Christmas tree? If that's the case, then I want my money back. I don't want to smell like a damned evergreen."

"You mean you haven't been spraying yourself with car freshener in lieu of cologne?" she deadpanned.

"Er, no."

She hummed doubtfully. "Live or artificial?" she asked.

"Live or artificial what?" He sounded confused.

"Christmas tree, of course. What do you think we're talking about?"

He laughed again, the sound low and strangely soothing. It moved through her and settled warmly around her heart. "I thought we were talking about the way I smell, but clearly you've moved on." He waited a beat. "A live branch. I do the Charlie Brown kind of Christmas tree."

"Ah. Is that a family tradition?"

She felt him stiffen beneath her and marveled at the change. She'd wanted to keep things light and noncommittal. Talking about Christmas had seemed like a safe topic, but clearly... not.

"Not really," he said, expelling a breath. "To be honest, I don't have any family. My father died several years ago and I've never known my mother or any of her family. Dad's parents passed before I was born."

He'd never known his mother? Meaning what? That she'd died when he was little? But if that was the case, then that's what he would have said, right? And he hadn't. He'd said he'd never known her. So if she hadn't died...then she must have left. Callous, selfish, miserable bitch. That explained a lot, Layla thought. Talk about hitting the motherlode of abandonment issues. Her chest gave a painful squeeze. "Sorry, Bryant. I don't know what to say."

"It's not your fault," he told her. "It just is and I've never known any different, so it's not a big deal."

Yes it was, but he'd never admit it. He couldn't even admit it to himself. She came this close to inviting him to her own family gathering, just to prevent him from being alone, but didn't. Something told her he'd reject the invitation out of hand and he would know that it had been issued out of pity. That would be reason enough to refuse.

"The family thing isn't all it's cracked up to be, you know," she said, determined to make light of what had become a very heavy moment.

"So I've been told."

"It's true. My mother's always freaking out over the dinner—is the stuffing too dry? Did she make enough desserts? Is everyone going to like their presents? Meanwhile, Dad is pulling enough electricity to power a Third World country to run his Christmas lights. He's adding a snowman village and insists that we do a living nativity every year."

"Living nativity?"

"Yep. And while I appreciate the sentiment, I don't particularly like freezing my ass off while playing Mary."

Bryant looked down at her, a grin twitching his lips. "Is this event open to the public?"

"Unfortunately, yes," she admitted drolly. "From six to nine on Christmas Eve, the Cole family front lawn." Rita would be home this year, which would make it all the more special.

His eyes twinkled. "Do I need tickets?"

"It's free to the public. Mom will make hot chocolate."

"I'll bring my own chestnuts," Bryant said.

She circled his nipple with her fingertip. "Bring a few for me, would you? I love chestnuts."

"You do?"

"Who doesn't?"

He paused. "I've planted trees," he told her. There was a bizarre note to his voice, one she couldn't quite discern.

"What?" For reasons she couldn't begin to explain, her heartbeat quickened and her mouth went dry.

"You asked about family traditions. We never really had what you would call a tradition, but my dad loved chestnuts. He'd roast them and turn on Bing Crosby. A couple of years ago I planted a small grove of trees on my farm. It'll be three to five more years before I can harvest, but I have to admit that I'm looking forward to it."

She felt faint. "You've got a farm? You're a farmer?"

He laughed. "Well, I wouldn't say that. I haven't planted a damned thing besides those chestnut trees and the odd tomato plant when I'm not touring."

She grunted. She couldn't do anything else. Artist's soul, farmer's tendency. He'd planted something he didn't expect to harvest for several years. He was committed to his home, to his land.

He just couldn't commit to a woman.

Nothing could have made her sadder.

ONCE AGAIN HE WAS PRESENTED with an opportunity to tell her where he lived, that he was her neighbor. Or he would be very soon anyway.

And he didn't.

What the hell was wrong with him? Why didn't he want to tell her? What was making him hesitate? Was he afraid she'd change her mind about the property? Decide to plant her sweet peas somewhere else? Or was it the mere significance of her choosing property next to his own? She'd reluctantly shown him her scrapbook this afternoon on the bus. He knew how important building her house was to her, that she equated having her own bit of land as permanence. And had he grown up with her childhood, moving about on the bus over and over, he would have likely felt the same way. In a sense, he suspected he did, just for a slightly different reason. It had certainly made her aversion to the bus make sense, that was for damned sure.

Looking at that scrapbook, seeing every detail of what she wanted for her home, down to the last flower, shrub and tree, really put everything into perspective for him. She'd spent years planning this, hours upon hours scanning house plans and plant catalogues to find just what she was looking for. Every room had been laid out, every decoration, the placement of furniture, even the rugs on the floor. She'd left nothing out, hadn't forgotten a single thing.

She was not the type of woman who would abandon a child.

"I'm about to ask you the most intensely personal question in the history of the world," she warned.

Oh, hell. What would she want to know? Why hadn't he ever married? Had he ever been in love? How many children did he want? He chuckled darkly. "Thanks for the warning."

She paused dramatically. "What are you thinking?"

He laughed again and relief swept through him. "That *is* the most intensely personal question in the history of the world," he said, surprised to realize that it was true.

"Well?"

"I was thinking about you, actually, and how you hate the tour bus." He *had* been thinking about that earlier, so it wasn't technically a lie.

She slid her foot against his calf. "Ah, yes," she groaned. "I loathe the bus. Even listening to the road noise makes me nauseous. I can't tell you how glad I am that we're flying home."

"Oh, I think you can," he said, laughing. "I can hear it in your voice."

She rolled on top of him, settling her sex over the ridge of his arousal. She bent forward and licked a path up the side of his neck. "Can you hear anything else?" she asked huskily.

Soft womanly skin, moist heat against his dick. He was five seconds away from saying to hell with a condom.

"Suit up," she whispered against his ear. "I want you inside of me."

In a flash he'd done as she instructed, and a moment later, she was lowering herself, inch by precious inch, down on him. Her heat slowly enveloped him and he set his teeth so hard he was afraid he'd ground the enamel off.

She was killing him. And, judging from that cat-in-the-cream-pot smile drifting over her lips, she was enjoying it.

Damp blond curls, smooth concave belly, the flare of her womanly hips, pink nipples resting like little tinted puffs of whipped cream upon her breasts.

She was quite possibly the most beautiful creature he'd ever seen in his life. His chest ached from looking at her, tightened and squeezed until he was breathless and dizzy.

She rose up, lowered herself once more, and the exquisite action between their joined bodies startled his respiration into action.

She skimmed her fingers over his chest, marking each rib with a tip, seemingly mesmerized by the way he felt beneath her hands. "Your body is like a sexual playground," she murmured. "Like a swing, a slide and a merry-go-round all rolled into one."

He grinned up at her, palmed her breasts and thumbed her nipples, then flexed determinedly beneath her. "Then ride."

And she did.

8

HAVING BEEN SUFFICIENTLY distracted twice—once against the wall and once in the bathroom—Layla milked the final note of her final performance from her instrument, then casually strolled offstage. She'd done it, she thought. She'd played without once thinking of the audience. Bryant was standing off to the side, his arms crossed over his chest, the strangest expression on his face.

Bewildered, indulgent...and oddly tortured.

Curiously enough, she understood that.

Things would never work between them on a permanent basis. She'd known that. He'd all but told her that he didn't ever want to settle down. She'd agreed to the terms and she wouldn't embarrass herself by trying to prolong the inevitable. Bryant had laid everything out for her so that she could make an informed decision before she slept with him.

She'd made the decision—she would accept the outcome.

That didn't mean she would have to like it, because she didn't. She hated that it was over between them before it had scarcely begun. Was she in love with him? Truthfully, she didn't know. She'd never been in love before. She had nothing to compare this to. Looking at him made her chest hurt, having him inside her made her feel that her bones were going to melt with happiness. She loved listening to the sound of his voice, appreciated his keen mind and sharp wit. His smile lit her up, made her want to smile, too.

Was that love?

It was something, and she hated walking away from it— from him. But she would do it because that was what was expected of her.

"That was beautiful, Layla," he said. "I might be biased, but I think Clint needs to forget Rusty and hire you on a permanent basis."

She was flattered, but hell, no, and she told him as much. "Don't you dare suggest that to him! I've been able to handle performing live because you've been distracting me—" her gaze tangled significantly with his "—but I'm not cut out for stage work."

He sidled closer. "I'd be happy to distract you all the time if you joined the band," he said.

"Take one for the team, eh?"

He laughed, searched her face. "Something like that."

She shook her head. "I don't think so. I'll build my house and stick to the studio."

He nodded and his expression said he'd expected as much. "Wanna play Scrabble?" he asked, jerking his head toward the game.

No. She wanted to sneak out to the bus and make love to him again. She wanted to ask him to come to Christmas dinner with her family, then ask him to come home with her and make s'mores in her living room fireplace. She wanted to see him in her house and in her bed because she knew he "fit," because she knew he belonged. But until he figured that out—and she was prepared for the hurtful fact that he probably never would—there was nothing she could do.

Instead, she blinked away the moisture in her eyes and the ache in her chest and said, "Sure."

And the last word she played was *bittersweet*.

TELLING HIMSELF THAT HE was the master of his destiny, that he wasn't going to be like his father, that what they'd had was wonderful but couldn't possibly be sustained, Bryant followed Layla to her car at the Nashville airport under the guise of making sure she wasn't attacked.

In truth, he didn't want to be away from her and was dreading the moment when she would get in her car and drive off, when the contact would be lost.

He grimly suspected a part of him would be lost as well.

She turned and smiled up at him, but the grin was frayed around the edges and didn't quite reach her eyes. "Here I am," she said, clicking her doors open with the keyless remote. To his surprise she drove a truck.

He grunted. "I pictured you in something a little more sporty."

She stepped out of the way while he stowed her bags. "This is more practical," she said. "I hated asking my dad every time I found something I needed to haul home."

That made sense. Little Miss Independent. He managed a grin. "Guess it'll come in handy when you're bringing all those flats of flowers home, huh?"

Another pained smile. "Yep."

He studied her for a moment, wishing he could say the words that would allow this to last, to keep her near.

But he knew better. People left. And it hurt. Instead, he leaned forward and pressed his lips to hers, lingered longer than he should. "Merry Christmas, Layla," he murmured.

He felt her grin against his lips. "You, too, Bryant. Good night."

She slid quickly into her car and pulled away into the night.

A hollow feeling settled in the pit of his belly, one he instinctively knew was going to last for a long time.

LAYLA DASHED A TEAR FROM her cheek and allowed herself one last look in the rearview mirror before making the turn that would take her out toward the interstate. He was still standing there, looking more like a lost little boy than a badass security agent.

It killed her to leave him, made something in her soul screech and howl.

But this was the way he wanted it. *He'd* made the rules. *He* had to be the one to change them.

This was not a choice she could make for him, and until he decided to choose her, to take a chance with her, there was nothing she could do but get used to the pain.

Merry Christmas, indeed.

9

HE WAS A GLUTTON FOR punishment, Bryant thought as he made his way slowly down Layla's parents' street. An idiot. A moron. A fool. But while he was being foolish...

It had taken the private investigator he'd hired yesterday less than three hours to find his grandparents. His grandfather was buried in The Willows Eternal Rest Cemetery less than sixty miles from where he lived, and his grandmother was in an assisted-living nursing home within five miles of where her husband was buried. Under the guise of visiting from an area church, Bryant had gone to meet Elsie Walker. Thin and withered with perfectly coifed snowy-white hair and bright pink lipstick, his grandmother wasn't the cookie-baking type granny he'd imagined. She was erect and regal, and while age had worn down her body, it had not dimmed her mind.

She'd taken one look at him and known he wasn't who he said he was. "You look very familiar, young man," she said. "I feel I should know you, but don't."

"I have that kind of face."

"Maybe so, but you have my daughter's eyes. What was your name again?"

He'd told her, and after she'd extracted a promise from him that he would visit again the following week, he'd left.

Elsie Walker had some pictures she'd like to show him, she'd explained. Mostly she'd talked about her husband, whom she'd loved dearly. Staying power might not have been a genetic trait passed on from either of his parents, but it was reassuring to see that his grandparents had had it. Fifty-seven years, all of them happy, she'd proudly told him. She hadn't much to say about her daughter, and Bryant suspected that, like him, Elsie hadn't heard from her in years.

What the hell was he doing here? Bryant wondered as he looked for a place to park on the street. The sidewalk was full and cars were lined up on either side of the road for half a block.

The truth was…he couldn't stay away. It had been little over twenty-four hours since he'd left Layla and it had felt like twenty-three hours fifty-nine minutes and fifty-nine seconds too long. Could he breathe without her? Yes.

But he didn't want to.

He had no idea where this was going or whether or not it would end in disaster. He didn't know if he could commit to a woman long-term, because he'd never tried—he'd never met a woman who'd inspired him to attempt it.

He wasn't altogether certain he was inspired now…but he couldn't stay away from her.

That's why he was here, in her town, on her street, hoping to catch a glimpse of her.

Pathetic, but he didn't care.

He slid in behind a sleek Lexus, exited the car and pocketed his keys. Shoulders hunched in his black peacoat against the cool Christmas Eve air, he followed the crowd on the sidewalk, waiting for his turn.

And there she was.

She was wrapped in a blue cloak, her blond hair covered by a hood, holding a squirming baby that was too big to be the infant Jesus, and looked largely entertained by all that was going on around him. It was the goat that held the child's attention, Bryant realized, following the kid's chubby pointing finger. Layla smiled and murmured something to the little boy, and as though she'd felt Bryant's stare, she turned her head and looked directly at him.

She smiled then, a genuinely happy-to-see-him grin that made the bottoms of his feet tingle and his chest warm. Her older sister, sensing Layla's preoccupation, followed her gaze, and the youngest one, Rita, gasped. She leaned over, and though he couldn't hear what she said, he knew she was asking Layla what he was doing here.

Layla handed the baby off, gestured to another cloaked woman waiting in the wings, then picked through the audience and made her way to him. "Bryant," she said wonderingly. "What are you doing here?"

Hell if he knew, Bryant thought, soaking her in. She had a freckle to the left of her nose. How had he missed that? He shrugged. "I was curious." *I wanted to see you. I couldn't stay away.*

She turned and looked at her family. "Pretty cool, isn't it?"

It was, so he nodded. He shifted, suddenly nervous. "Look, I know that you've got your family thing tomorrow, but I was wondering if your evening would be free."

She turned back to face him. "My evening?"

This was harder than he'd thought it would be. He'd never invited anyone to share the holiday with him before, but he wanted her there. "I thought we could have some eggnog, roast some chestnuts over an open fire."

"At your house?"

"Yeah." This was a mistake, Bryant thought. He shouldn't have asked her. She would come out of pity, because she knew he was going to be alone. Dammit, why—

A slow-dawning smile slid over her lips. "I would love to."

His world brightened. "Really?"

"Really."

"I'll text directions to your phone," he said. "See you around seven then?"

"I'll be there with bells on."

He didn't care what she wore, so long as she showed up.

LORD, PLEASE DON'T LET me be in an accident or get pulled over, Layla silently prayed as she made her way out to Bryant's place. She was wearing a long coat and little else and was currently debating the wisdom of such a choice. It had seemed like a good idea at the time. It had been too late to get Bryant a proper present, but with some leftover Christmas decorations, she'd turned herself into one.

Now she felt ridiculous.

Incidentally, she hadn't needed directions to his place. She'd taken one look at the address—Hardscrabble Road—and instantly understood that sly little smile he'd worn when she'd told him about her land.

He was her neighbor. Or would be, very soon.

She couldn't imagine why he hadn't simply told her. Had their positions been reversed, she wouldn't have been able to stand not telling him. But Bryant...

She couldn't get a bead on Bryant. Just when she was certain she had him completely figured out, that their relationship was destined to explode like a fantastic firework and disappear just as quickly, he'd shown up at her parents' and asked her to Christmas.

She was trying not to read too much into this—he didn't want to be alone, he wasn't finished with her yet, etc.—but she couldn't seem to help herself. Something about him just clicked for her. He felt right. More importantly, she felt right when she was with him.

Anxiety tightened her belly into a miserable knot as she spied his mailbox and turned down his driveway. His house wasn't visible from the road, but lights shone in the distance.

Her mouth formed a silent O as she found herself in the circular driveway in front of his house. It was a small cabin with a screened-in front porch. Golden light spilled from the windows and smoke curled from the chimney. All it needed was a blanket of snow to be Thomas Kinkade picturesque.

And then he was there, in the doorway, and the smile that split his face as she hurried up the walk—socks, why hadn't she worn socks?—made her chest fill with warm fuzzy air.

"Hey, you," he said, pulling her inside and immediately into his arms.

And this was home, she realized. It wasn't a house or a piece of property. It was here, in his arms. Layla quaked with the realization.

"You're cold," he said, drawing back with concern. "Come over by the fire and let's see if I can warm you up."

Oh, she knew he could do that. She followed him on shaky legs, taking in a bit of his decor along the way. Wide-plank pine floors, comfortable furniture, art—no doubt his own—and high-end electronics. The kitchen and dining area were open to the living room and the ceilings soared overhead, giving the impression of additional space. She liked it, she thought. It suited him.

"Here, let me get your coat," he offered.

She faked a shiver. "I'll leave it on for a minute more, if you don't mind."

He gave her an odd look. "Sure. How was the day with your family?"

She settled onto his couch and rolled her eyes. "Hectic. Wonderful. The same as it always is."

"That's nice."

"What about your day?" she asked.

His gaze warmed. "It just got better."

So had hers. "What have you been doing?"

He pulled a small wrapped box from the coffee table and handed it to her. "Making you something."

Touched, Layla felt her eyes widen. "Bryant, you didn't have to do that. I didn't expect—"

"I wanted to," he said simply. "Open it."

She did, carefully. A tree pendent, a bit smaller than the one he wore, was nestled in a swath of scrap fabric. She gasped and withdrew it, holding it up to the light so that she could get a better look. "It's beautiful," she breathed. "Thank you."

"I included the roots, because I knew they were important to you."

She swallowed tightly. "I see that."

She didn't know when any gift had ever meant more to her. Her eyes glistened. "It's perfect."

He slid a finger beneath her eye, catching a tear. "You're perfect."

"What am I doing here, Bryant?" she asked, because she had to know. Needed to know what he was thinking. "I didn't figure you wanted this."

He shook his head. "I didn't, either. But I can't get you out of my head, Layla. And I don't want to. I don't know where this is going. I don't know if I can be that guy, the one you want, but I know that I'll regret it for the rest of my life if I don't try." He laced his fingers through hers and gave her hand a significant squeeze. "I just know that I'm grounded when I'm with you. Centered. *Rooted.* And I like that."

It was as close to a declaration of love as she was going to get, and since she wasn't ready to declare herself yet either, that was fine.

She nodded, in full understanding, then smiled. "Would you like to unwrap your present?" she asked.

"You brought me something?"

"It's not new," she said. He'd had her before, but...

"That doesn't matter."

She guided his hand to the belt at her waist and helped him

untie the sash. The coat fell open, revealing red and green plaid Christmas bows on her breasts and a large velvet bow—complete with a silver bell—over her hoo-ha. She'd made a thong for the occasion. Being crafty had its perks.

His eyes darkened and she watched him lick his lips. "You are the best Christmas present I have ever gotten, hands down."

Layla smiled, pulled a piece of mistletoe from her coat pocket and dangled it over his head, then bent forward and kissed him. "Unwrap me."

* * * * *

A BABE IN TOYLAND
Tawny Weber

To Rhonda Nelson and Kate Hoffmann—
two awesomely fun ladies to work with!
Thanks for making this such a great experience.

"IF ONE MORE GUY OFFERS to jingle my bells, I'm going to dump a pitcher of beer over his happy-holidaying head."

"'Tis the season, goodwill toward drunken men, and all that." Rita Cole winked at the other waitress before shifting a glass-filled tray from her shoulder to the teak bar. Bright lights, chrome and flowering vines were supposed to make the Asbury Park yuppie bar welcoming and innocuous. But the goody-goody decor didn't hide the meat-market vibe.

"Consider it a gift," Rita suggested. Life was hard enough without getting uptight over petty stuff. And any guys haunting this bar were inevitably going to be petty. "They get a few harmless fantasies and you get a sweet tip. Everyone's happy."

"Speaking of happy," Kimmi said as she counted change, "thanks again for hooking me up with that pediatrician. How on earth did you find a baby doc?"

"I met her when I was apprenticing at the Hershberger salon in Manhattan. She was one of Sally's clients."

"How does a girl with all your skills and connections end up schlepping drinks in a bar?" the blonde asked as she hefted her own tray.

Wasn't that the question of the hour? And one Rita wasn't

about to try to answer without a pitcher of margaritas, a box of tissues and a pile of chocolate to stave off the depression.

Instead, she forced herself to smile. There was no way she could spend eight hours with her feet wrapped in stiletto boots and her butt barely covered by a fur-trimmed velvet skirt if she was in a bad mood. Besides, a good mood meant better tips.

And she desperately needed the money.

She'd learned a long time ago that when a girl resembled a Playboy centerfold—all curves and wickedly sultry looks, guys looked whether she liked it or not. Given the choice between hiding her assets or making the most of them, she'd take the ogling. She just wished she could leave the judgment that went with it behind.

Five minutes later, her resolve was tested. She had just deposited a chocolatini, two margaritas and a pitcher of beer at a table of ladies and collected their credit cards when she felt a fat-fingered hand slide up the back of her thigh, skimming the hem of her short skirt.

When she spun around the hand dropped, but the guy's smirk didn't. Her stomach tensed but she forced herself to keep her smile intact.

"Sorry, were you wanting to place an order?" she asked as she subtly shifted her now-empty tray into a weapon-worthy position. "I can recommend Paul's coffee if you need some help sobering up."

"Screw coffee—I'd rather have a buttery nipple," the pudgy guy said with a sloppy grin. "Better yet, why don't you sit down here on my lap and let me taste yours?"

His companions, all equally take-their-keys-away drunk, laughed uproariously. Paul, the bartender, caught Rita's eye and raised a brow in question. A quick shake of her head let him know she could handle it. She'd been doing so half her life.

Why was it some jerks looked at her and saw easy? She

knew she put off a sexy vibe, but sexy and disrespect didn't go hand in hand. She leaned forward to ask why the hell he thought her looks gave him permission to grab her ass. Then she took a deep breath. What was the point?

"How about I bring you that coffee on the house," she offered instead. After all, there was a tip on the line.

"How about I show you my candy cane," the guy leered. Then he lurched forward to grab her again.

Screw the tip. She shifted sideways so his arm slammed into the table. Just before she blasted him, Rita heard her mother's voice in her head. *Try a little honey before you lose your temper.*

So she sucked in a deep breath, reined in her irritation and refocused. She glanced across the table and arched her brow at the drunk's buddies.

"A good-lookin' bunch of guys like you, letting him ruin your chances with the ladies?" She shifted her gaze, taking in the group of women watching from the table she'd just served. She leaned in closer, speaking in a loud whisper. "Nothing more impressive than a guy who comes to the rescue."

Forcing herself to keep her smile in place, Rita waited. Their responses dulled by booze, the drunk's companions eventually clued in. They exchanged glances, then one of the guys reached over and smacked the drunk on the shoulder.

"Dude, you're being rude. Apologize and pay the sexy...I mean, pay the nice waitress."

Their drunk friend looked belligerent. Rita balanced on the balls of her feet, just in case. But the guy's buddies, so focused on posturing for the ladies, glared. One even half stood, flexing.

Finally the drunk's frown shifted into a hardy, slightly embarrassed laugh. One eye on his pals, he handed over a twenty to pay for his five-dollar drink and told Rita to keep the change. His friends quickly followed suit before moving their chairs around to flirt with the women at the next table.

"And that's how it's done," Rita murmured to Kimmi as they passed again, pretending her heart wasn't hammering with leftover nerves.

"Maybe for you," Kimmi shot back. "You go through life like it's a big ol' party."

"Networking at its finest," Rita claimed as she tucked the tip into her bra and tried to reclaim her upbeat mood.

"With your looks and people skills, you'll be waitress of the month in no time," Kimmi said, gesturing to the photo wall. "It's hokey, but you do get a hundred-dollar bonus."

"Nope, I'm not sticking around that long," Rita told her. "Not even for a C-note. Humoring drunks isn't one of my career goals." Even if it was the job she ended up doing ninety percent of the time. "I'm just here to get enough money to pay for my trip home to Ponder Hill for the holidays."

Kimmi's grimace said it all.

Home. Holidays. Family.

Ugh.

Exactly.

Still, loyalty had Rita saying, "It'll be great. I haven't been home for Christmas in years."

"You like your family?"

"Yeah," Rita said, shifting to take some weight off her left foot, then her right. "Yeah, actually they're all great. Perfect, in fact."

Which was why Rita had never quite fit in. The only thing she was perfect at was being a pain in the ass. After a while, seeing that look in her parents' eyes, that *where did we go wrong* look, got to be too much. It was easier to stay away than to deal with their disappointment.

Over the years she'd made excuses at the holidays or talked one of her sisters into suggesting a family trip instead.

Until this year. After six Christmases, her mom had insisted Rita come home. Apparently, without her presence, her father's holiday would be ruined. Amanda insisted that without all three of his daughters around the tree, her husband would sink into depression.

What choice did Rita have? She was pretty sure it was mostly bullshit, but how could she risk her father's happiness at the holidays?

"Perfect, huh?" Kimmi made a face. "Is that why you look so thrilled?"

"Well, let's just say I was much happier about the prospect when I originally gave in…I mean, agreed to go home."

Before her latest career bust. Her sixth since leaving home at eighteen, which only added to her parents' readily shared worries. Unshared, she was sure, were their suspicions that she was a total loser.

A suspicion she was starting to buy into.

Case in point. She'd loved the idea of being in fashion. She was great at putting together outfits. But as her most recent boss, a high-end clothing designer had reluctantly told her, she had a narrow vision and a quirky style that only one percent of the population could pull off. In other words, she sucked as a designer.

Her big plan for the holidays had been to prove to her parents that she wasn't their loser little girl. Part one was to wow them with tales of her career success. Part two had been to get them an awesome present, like her sisters always did. She'd prove that she was not only focused and happy, but that she was doing well enough to buy them something they'd never forget.

And she'd found the perfect gift. The lady who ran the antiques shop in Ponder Hill had tracked down an antique victrola just like Rita's great-granny's. Rita had grown up hearing the story of how her parents, both musicians, had loved to dance to music from that antique victrola while dating. When Rita was about two, her dad had broken it during one of their many moves.

She'd been so excited to find one. This was a gift that would not only outdo her sisters', but touch her parents' hearts. She'd spent the past six months making payments, with the last installment due when she got home to pick it up.

A payment she no longer had, thanks to losing her job and having to use her savings to pay rent.

But she wasn't giving up. She had a Plan B.

Wait tables, smile until her cheeks hurt, and pull in enough tips to make up the lost funds. Squaring her shoulders to shake off her doubts, Rita lifted another tray of drinks and turned to weave expertly through the crowd. She'd only gone a couple feet when she saw the key to Plan B belly up to the bar.

"Benny, you cutie pie. Get yourself a drink on me and I'll be with you in a few." She gave the pudgy balding guy an extra big smile and winked as she turned away. She needed Benny to agree to put off their departure by a few extra days to give her some time to sock away more money. She hoped smiles and the sight of her ass in a short skirt would do the trick.

On cue, he immediately zeroed in on her legs.

While Benny enjoyed his thrill, the guy behind him caught her eye. A tiny shiver of awareness slid down her belly, then the crowd moved and she lost the view. Crazy. Even though she rarely dated these days, hot guys were still pretty common in her life, but they rarely gave her tingles. Not even tall, sexy guys with wind-tossed golden hair and shoulders to die for.

"Cutie pie?" Kimmi shot back. "You need your eyes checked."

"Looks aren't everything," Rita said dismissively. "He's from Ponder Hill. Benny graduated with my oldest sister, and when I put the word out that I was looking for a ride, he offered a no-strings-attached transport home for the holidays."

"Ooh?"

Rita snickered at the sexy lilt in Kimmi's tone but shook her head. "Hardly. In the first place, he's a nice guy but not my type."

Her dream type had been cemented back in high school. Tall, bad-boy blond with a chip on his shoulder and an attitude that said *c'mon*. Rita sighed at the memory. She'd met plenty of bad boys, plenty of blonds and plenty of guys with attitude. But none did it for her like that wild Ramsey boy had.

"And in the second place?" Kimmi urged.

Rita gave a rueful half smile and said, "In the second place, Benny's a mama's boy. And I'm hardly the kind of girl guys bring home to their family."

TYLER RAMSEY WATCHED the sexy pinup queen make her way through the crowd, noting his weren't the only eyes glued to the sweet curve of her ass. Rita Cole. Pure fantasy material and the last woman in the world Tyler wanted to see.

"C'mon, Benny," Tyler cajoled. "You've got better things to do than play taxi to a diva. Tell her the deal's off and let's go test your new bike." He referred to the custom Harley he'd driven fourteen freaking hours to deliver. To a guy who, instead of showing the brand-new bike off to all the potential customers he'd told Tyler about, was taking off in the morning to drive those same fourteen hours back to Ponder Hill. Hell, if Tyler had known, he'd have stayed home and let Benny get the bike there.

He definitely wouldn't have gotten within touching distance of Rita Cole.

Tyler was pretty sure every damned mistake man had ever made could be laid at one of the Cole sisters' sexy toes.

"Better things to do?" Benny breathed, his eyes glued on Rita's fluffy white hem. "No way. This is my shot. My golden opportunity. My—"

"A waste of your time. A waste of gas money. And the pain of having to watch all those sexy wet dreams dry up when you have to admit what she really is."

That got Benny's attention. He glared. Between the light

glinting off his bald head and reflecting off his Coke-bottle glasses, he looked like a pissed-off, myopic holiday elf.

Tyler winced with guilt. Ever since grade school, nerdy Benny had followed Tyler around, content to hang in his friend's shadow. A perfect example was the guy contracting Tyler to build him a Harley. Benny the nerd on a Harley, just to help his old buddy launch his new business. That was friendship.

The only time Benny didn't listen to Tyler was when it came to women. The guy was a sucker for women out of his league, never able to see past the packaging.

While their packaging was top-notch, the Cole sisters were bad news. Rita had gone to high school with Tyler's little brother, Randy. Gone to school with him, gone out with him, gone done and broke his damned heart. You'd think the kid would've caught a clue from Tyler's experience with Rita's older sister, Alison. But, no. There was something irresistible about those girls.

Alison Cole had been Tyler's senior prom date. He'd had a secret crush on Rita, but even a bad boy like Tyler couldn't ask a freshman to prom. So he'd asked Alison instead, then spent part of the evening passing a flask with his buddies. Combine too much whiskey, Alison's perfume and a pathetic attempt at the Macarena and the night had been a mess. Especially when, after they'd gone out for air, he'd puked all over her prom dress, then passed out. The next thing he knew, everyone in school was whispering that he'd knocked Alison up.

His rep had been trashed. His face had almost got smashed by her angry father. He'd spent four weeks in detention for fighting with every guy who'd had the nerve to ridicule him when the truth had come out. Alison had started the rumor herself to get revenge for his ruining her evening.

He'd vowed to avoid all of the Cole girls from then on.

So at the moment, he didn't know what pissed him off more. The trouble the sisters caused? Or that, even though he knew better, just the sight of Rita Cole turned him on like crazy.

"She's trouble, buddy. I just don't want to see you hurt."

"Don't talk about her like that," Benny snapped. "Rita's gorgeous. She's the one, you know. The future Mrs. Rodgers. I've been waiting for this chance for years."

Benny rambled on about her beauty and perfection, showing some scary hints of obsession. Tyler wasn't sure if the guy even saw her as a person or as a walking, talking blow-up doll.

Years of accumulated frustration, not all of it sexual, boiled over when Rita, squeezing between bodies to slide her tray onto the bar, gave Benny a quick hug.

Tyler's body hit automatic meltdown. God, she was gorgeous. A sexy combination of a forties' pinup girl and a sweet girl-next-door, she'd filled his dreams for almost a decade now. He'd only seen her twice in the past eight years, and now she was right next to him. Close enough to reach out and run his fingers through her tousled black hair. To see if her skin was as silky smooth as it looked. To taste her full lips.

As if echoing his thoughts, Benny's pleasured groan was the last straw. Tyler had to get the guy to give up his obsession. Maybe then he could finally give up his, too.

His body overruling his brain, Tyler stepped around Benny and wrapped an arm around Rita's surprisingly fragile shoulders. Pulling her to his side, he gave himself three seconds to enjoy the twin thrills of her surprise and his own lust. He reveled in the feel of her lush curves pressing into his chest, her shocked breath wafting over his lips as she gasped.

Then he made his move.

"Hey Rita, nice to see you again," he said before taking her mouth in a slippery, hot, wet and wild kiss.

2

THIS WAS WHAT DROWNING in lust must feel like. Waves of passion poured over Rita, overwhelming her senses with excitement. She tried to catch her breath, but her mouth was too busy playing slippery-slide against a pair of deliciously erotic lips.

Her body melted as molten heat swirled. Jellylike, her legs buckled. Rita had never had a kiss like this. Never. A single hands-free, fully dressed kiss and she could taste the edge of a hot, wild orgasm.

Wanting—needing—more, she pressed tight against the hard, well-sculpted chest and moaned.

It wasn't until someone tugged at her arm that she realized she'd lost her mind. Kissing a total stranger. At work. Insane. Barely cognizant of the whoops and whistles, Rita slowly pulled back to stare up into blue eyes she recognized from her naughtiest secret dreams.

Tyler? Tyler Ramsey? No way. Had Santa come early?

"What the hell d'ya think you're doing?" Benny yelped, his voice breaking through the sex haze fogging Rita's mind.

"Benny…" She trailed off, not sure what she wanted to say since her brain was still stuttering.

"You…he…how could you…?" Benny babbled, his eyes huge behind thick lenses.

The hurt in his glare made her realize that she was still plastered against the best kisser her mouth had ever encountered. Her breath shuddered when she forced herself to peel her breasts off his chest. Rita took two steps back and blinked a few times, trying to shake off the fog of lust.

"Tyler Ramsey?" she breathed, her eyes as big as Benny's. "What the hell are you doing here?"

"Screwing me over's what he's doing," Benny growled.

"C'mon, Ben, you saw for yourself how that went down," Tyler drawled, shoving one hand through the sandy hair that had fallen over his sky-blue eyes. "All I did was prove my point."

"What point?" Rita asked, her back going up at the dismissal in Tyler's voice. She tried to ignore the familiar pain, but, dammit, she recognized that tone. It was the same one he'd always used when referencing her.

"You betrayed me," the little guy whined, glaring at her. Then he turned the evil eye on Tyler. "Fine. You want her? Then you can take her home."

"Huh?" *Betrayed?*

Ignoring her, the men faced off. Tyler reached out as if to give Benny a calming pat on the head at the same time that Benny swung his fist.

"Aw, Ben," he said with a wince as they all watched Benny miss, thumping a huge bruiser of a guy in the back of the head instead of Tyler. Furious, the man turned. His gaze slid past Benny as if he wasn't even there, landing accusingly on Tyler instead.

With a sigh, Tyler ducked the guy's massive punch. Coming up, fists swinging and wearing a huge grin, he proved his hometown rep as an ass-kicker was still valid when he dove into the brawl.

Yelping, Rita barely made it back against the bar before

the fight went viral. Grunts and crunching groans sounded over the taunting cheers of the onlookers.

Ten minutes, a bloody lip and a few broken bar stools later, Tyler finished his chat with the local cops. Rita's boss stood in the still-crowded space, looking furious under his Santa hat. While he chewed Tyler out, Rita tried to calm a sputtering Benny.

"Look, blame it on the mistletoe," Tyler interrupted Larson's lecture. "It's no big. I'll pay for damages. Kissing Rita was worth every penny."

"What?" In the middle of assuring Benny that Tyler had just been saying hi and didn't mean anything by the kiss, Rita turned to stare into her longtime crush's sexy blue eyes. She saw the desire battling with amusement there, and couldn't hold back an answering smile. "Worth every penny, hmm?"

She hadn't meant to sound so flirtatious, but she couldn't help it. Tyler Ramsey always made her feel she had something to prove. But her comments were the final straw for Benny. He threw up his puny arms as if shouting *betrayal,* and stormed out. Rita's protest was lost on his departing back.

"Miss Cole, were you the center of this altercation?"

It suddenly hit home just what that kiss had cost her. Rita's lust melted fast as she glared at Tyler. He wiped his swollen lip with the back of his hand and grinned. Desperate, she gave her boss a hopeful little smile and tried to BS her way out of the mess.

"Now Mr. Larson, you know how these things go…"

"Are you trying to say you were innocent?"

Tyler's snort of laughter made Rita grind her teeth.

"You know the rules, Miss Cole," Larson shot back, not waiting for her answer. "Get your personal effects and meet me upstairs in ten minutes. I'll have your final wages prepared."

Ignoring her protests, as well as the echoing arguments from the surrounding waitresses and the bartender, the manager swept through the crowd toward a door marked Private. Fighting off despair, Rita watched him go. Then she sucked in a breath deep enough to make Tyler's eyes glint in heated appreciation.

"I hope you're happy," she muttered. "You couldn't just say hello like a normal person?"

"I thought you liked the kiss." Looking just as cocky as he had when he'd raided the girls' locker room, Tyler leaned his hip on a bar stool and gave her his patented *aw, shucks* smile.

"That kiss wasn't worth the spilled beer," she lied.

"Sweetheart, you're breaking my heart."

"I'd like to break your head," she snapped. He'd ruined everything. She needed this job, dammit. She had to get home. She remembered how he'd ruined her sister's prom and glared at him. Obviously Tyler was living proof of once a gorgeous, sexy jerk, always a gorgeous, sexy jerk.

Then, eyes narrowing, she dug her fists into the velvety fabric of her skirt. "But instead, I'm going to let you make it all better."

Tyler's smile took on a wicked edge. His gaze cruised her curves.

"All better, how?" he murmured, his meltingly flirtatious stare sweeping over her like a tingling caress.

Rita ignored it. She'd be damned if he'd fog her brain with sex thoughts. His eyes traced the curve of her breasts beneath the tight red top, sending a shaft of heat spiraling deep in her belly. Okay, so she'd settle for not letting him know he'd fogged her brain.

Plan B was kaput, so she needed her wits to develop a Plan C. And fast.

"You not only got me fired, Tyler, you lost me my way home."

Before he could do more than wince, Rita was up in his

face, toe to toe as she drilled one red-tipped finger into his chest. And she hoped like hell it hurt.

"You heard Benny," she said, despite the sick feeling in her stomach. The solution she'd come up with wasn't one she liked, but it was all she had. "You caused this problem and he told you exactly how to fix it."

"What the hell are you talking about?"

"I'm talking about the fact that you just volunteered to be my escort home for the holidays."

CARTING THE LAST BIN to the door, Rita brushed her bangs out of her eyes with her shoulder and blew out a breath. A childhood on the road while her musician parents performed bluegrass, plus her own inability to settle in one place, made moving second nature. A half-dozen plastic storage bins, a couple suitcases and her tote bag and she was ready to roll.

She dropped the bin on top of the hand truck and frowned at the random cardboard box next to her things.

"Shawn? What's this?" she yelled to her soon-to-be ex-roommate. Shawn trudged out, a huge mug of coffee almost hiding her face.

"S'my present to you," the petite brunette said around a yawn. "I know you didn't make enough to cover that last payment on your 'rents gift, so I figured this'd help out."

Rita eyed the box. It was half the size of her storage bins, hardly big enough to hold an antique record player. "Is it like a do-it-yourself thing?" she joked, poking at the cardboard.

Shawn choked on her coffee. Laughing, she wiped her chin and patted the box. "How'd you guess?"

Eyes narrowed, Rita flipped a glance from the box to Shawn to the darkened window. It was a quarter to five in the morning—the time she'd told Tyler to pick her up. Did she have time to play games? Then again, what were the chances that he'd really show?

"So what is it? A new toy?" she asked, peeking out the window.

Not that she was anxious or anything. Tyler Ramsey was a first-class jerk, albeit one helluva gorgeous first-class jerk. But gorgeous didn't matter, because he was just a means to an end. Plan C.

She pressed her hand to her belly to settle the dancing nerves. Just because he'd knocked her on her ass with those magic lips of his didn't mean she was itching to see him again. She hadn't even put makeup on, proof positive that she wasn't looking to make an impression.

If he showed up, that was. Which he probably wouldn't.

"More like toys," Shawn said, pulling Rita's attention back to the mystery box with a gesture to open it.

Rita tugged up the flaps, then frowned. She shook the box, staring at the colorful array of vibrators, cock rings and God knew what else as they tumbled together. Mouth dragging the floor, she gave her roommate a shocked stare.

"What the…?"

Shawn poked her fingernail at a neon green rubber dildo. "They're discontinued toys. Last year's models, overstocks, a few rejects. There's a product guide in there I printed with their names, features, retail price. Should be all you need."

Rita goggled, actually goggled. What the hell?

Her gaze bounced from Shawn's sleepy face to the box of misfit sex toys. "I'm out of a job, homeless and heading to my parents' for some holiday humiliation. And you're giving me…the promise of satisfaction?" She glanced at the contents of the box again and added, "Over and over again?"

Shawn smirked. "If that's how you want it, sure. I figured you could, you know, sell them. Like they do at those toy parties and stuff? These are free and clear," she assured Rita. Shawn owned an adult bookstore, and while she was a strong supporter of all things kink, she'd never do anything illegal.

"Look, if you won't take them as a present, take them as

an apology." Shawn stuffed her hands in her robe pockets and hunched her shoulders. "I hate that I can't hold the room for you. It's bad enough you're out of a job, but…"

"You need to make rent." Rita didn't want to add to Shawn's guilt. "And I appreciate the idea, I really do—"

"Don't refuse," Shawn interrupted. "Just, you know, think about it. If you decide the idea sucks, you can dump the box on the side of the road."

Rita snickered, not sure which amused her more. The image of some random traveler finding a box of neon dildos. Or the idea of heading home with the hunkiest man she'd ever lusted after, carrying her own arsenal of sex toys.

TYLER'S FINGERS RAPPED a fast rhythm on the steering wheel as he stared through the light dusting of snow at a dark apartment building. Tiny white lights shone from the lobby window, glinting off the red plastic bow on the door wreath.

What the hell was he doing? Guilt didn't work on him. He grimaced, shoulders hunching just a little. At least, it wasn't supposed to work on him. But Rita had been right. His being a jackass had caused her problems. So here he was, five o'clock in the morning, playing chauffeur.

He knew it was a huge mistake, yet he couldn't convince himself to leave. He owed her. Sure, driving her home was gonna piss Benny off all over again. And yes, once Tyler's own brother found out, Randy would join Benny in wanting to kick some ass. Yet he couldn't stop himself.

That was Rita Cole for you. From myopic Benny, who had no clue what she was like but worshipped her from afar, to gullible young Randy, who'd actually dated her back in high school and still carried a painful torch. Even Tyler himself had spent way too many teenage nights dreaming about her.

Teenage, hell—he'd tossed and turned all last night reliving that kiss. The feel of her soft lips, the sensation of her curves pressed against his body. Her scent, her taste. The way her eyes had gone all soft and sexy when she stared up at him as if he was the answer to her every desire.

Tyler dropped his head on the steering wheel and let it bounce a few times.

He had to get a grip.

And where was she? He glanced at the building again, then at his watch. Five more minutes and he was out of here. Even as he assured himself she wouldn't show up, a part of him, the part that had crushed on her for years, wondered what it'd be like to spend a couple days with Rita. To actually get to know her. To find out if that sweetness he'd always suspected was under the surface of her flirty looks was real or imagined.

Four minutes of enough reluctant fantasies to fog his windows and Tyler reached for the ignition. He couldn't take any more. He'd paid his debt by showing up. It was better for everyone that she'd blown him off.

As if she'd known his absolute limit, before he could turn the key there was a knock on the truck window. Tyler gave a manly effort to disguise his startled jump.

"Rita." Shit. Tyler told himself the surge rocketing through his system was irritation, not excitement. He stared, not sure what to make of the diva-turned-waif standing on the sidewalk. Unlike the woman he'd expected, she wasn't fluff-haired and paint-faced, or dressed in diva-wear. Her hair was a straight fall—black as night—to shoulders wrapped in a puffy red jacket that'd seen better days. Her skin was as pale as usual, but Tyler was pretty sure the dewy glow was natural, not cosmetic. Not a speck of glitter or leather in sight.

His brow furrowed as he stepped out of the truck. Where was the supersexy Rita he could lust after and dismiss?

"Good morning," she said with a bright smile that made him think more about hugging her than stripping her naked. Dammit. Then she gestured to a stack of storage containers piled on a dolly. "Wanna help me load these in the back?"

Not luggage, Tyler noted as his gut tightened. Boxes. Like she was moving back home.

Home, where his brother was. The brother who still talked about Rita as if she was the lost love of his life. Who claimed he'd never find true love because Rita had broken his heart. Who had laid blame for all his dating failures and almost bombing medical school at Rita's feet.

Tyler knew his little brother had a tendency to overreact. Half the time, he swore the kid would do better on the stage than in the hospital. But…he'd promised when their dad ran out twenty years back, that he'd always protect and look out for his family.

So no matter how overdramatic he might think Randy was, Tyler was still driving home the woman who'd caused all his little brother's misery.

Wasn't this going to be a merry freaking Christmas.

3

"LET'S SET A FEW GROUND rules before we hit the road," Tyler decided, desperately needing to get the upper hand. He had no idea what rules to set, though. *Don't seduce me* sounded a little pathetic.

"Haven't you heard? I don't do rules." Her anger was clear, even though her words were slurry with exhaustion. "And since I've spent the entire night packing because your cute little trick lost me not only my job, but my ability to pay rent, I am now going to take a nap."

Cute little trick? It took Tyler thirty whole seconds to realize she was referring to his kiss. Was she crazy? That lip-lock had been incendiary. The kind of stuff that burned down good intentions and leveled resistance. A move every guy in that bar had been fantasizing he could pull off.

Cute, his ass. He directed a glare her way before he realized it was pointless.

She'd tugged a pair of sunglasses over half her face and curled her body away from him, burrowing into the puffy red fabric of her coat. From the slow, even tenor of her breath, Tyler could tell she was already asleep.

Well, hell. Nothing to do but leave, he realized, pulling away from the curb. The GPS on his dash flashed the route, marking it fourteen hours and twelve minutes until they arrived in Ponder Hill.

Fourteen hours until Rita was in the same town as Randy. Randy who would throw a fit and ruin their mother's holiday.

Tyler glanced at the woman he'd always called a diva. She looked more like a worn-out waif, her bright red jacket contrasting her black hair and pale skin. She appeared to be out for a few hours, at least.

Good. That would give him time to come up with a plan. Something. Anything.

Maybe first, though, he should figure out how to get rid of this vague wish to curl up next to her, wrap her in his arms and bury his face in that silky hair.

THE SMELL OF FOOD SLOWLY seeped through the cozy blanket of sleep wrapped around Rita. She had a brief, lethargic mental debate about diving back into her dreams, but nothing grabbed her attention faster than deep-fried cooking.

With a little moan, she stretched her arms overhead, the cold glass of the passenger window sending shivers up her fingers. Uncurling her legs, she yawned and forced her eyes open. Even with sunglasses on, the overbright sunshine screamed *morning*. Squinting behind the dark lenses, she took in the view.

They were parked outside a truck stop, surrounded by chrome and steel. Tyler had shifted, so his back was against the door and one knee drawn up on the bench seat. The food, glorious greasy goodness, was spread on a takeout tray between them. Fries and onion rings, a couple burgers, hot pie, some fruit and even a green salad. Obviously Tyler wasn't an only-breakfast-in-the-morning kind of guy.

She wished that didn't add so much to his appeal.

"Good morning, sunshine," he drawled around a bite of

what looked like a double-bacon cheeseburger. "I didn't know what you liked, so I got a bit of everything."

Everything, indeed.

Overwhelmed and blaming her vulnerability on being fresh from sleep, she pulled her gaze away from the hypnotic depths of his blue eyes and glanced around.

Frowning, she looked at the clock on the dash. It was after eight and they weren't even out of New Jersey?

"What's up?" she asked, feeling a little defensive with her face naked and still soft from sleep. "You too busy watching me nap to put in the mileage?"

"What makes you think I was watching you?"

Rita gave him a wink and ran her fingers through her hair to wind it into a ponytail. "Because sleeping with me is a goal of men far and wide," she teased.

"How d'ya know you don't drool?" he asked.

Rita couldn't tell if he was flirting or not. Tyler came across as this laconic, rough-edged bad boy with a wicked sense of humor and an even more wicked right hook. But for all his good-ol'-boy charm, he was impossible to read.

"Me? Drool? No way." Sucking up the sweet punch of carbonated caffeine, she gave him an arch look. "I have plenty of references who'll swear otherwise."

Tyler's blue eyes narrowed, then took on a deliciously languorous look. The kind of look she figured he gave his bedmates just before a little morning tumble. Her stomach dipped down to her toes as she imagined waking up next to him. Beside him. On top of him.

He'd never given her that look before. She warned herself not to let it go to her head.

"I'm not the kind of guy who relies much on references. I'd rather decide for myself."

"Is that an invitation?" she asked in a low, wicked tone.

His grin was a slow work of art. She knew better than to

tumble at the sight of a wicked smile and sexy eyes, but man, oh man, her breath still hitched a little.

"If I issue an invitation, sweetheart, you won't have to clarify."

Taking a moment to replenish the breath in her lungs, Rita tried to calm her racing pulse and eject from her head the vivid images of the two of them sliding together in a naked dance.

"I'll make note of that," she murmured, pretending she wasn't cowed by reaching for some fruit instead of pursuing that intriguing line of thought.

"So, what's up?" she asked after she'd finished an orange and half the French fries. A balanced breakfast if she did say so herself. "I'm not criticizing, but why aren't we farther along?"

Something flickered in his eyes. Rita didn't know what, or why, but she felt her defenses rise.

"I've got a few stops to make on my way home. Some bike shops, a couple buddies who're interested in new rides."

Rita knew he was talking about the motorcycles he customized. He'd always been into bikes. It must be nice, she mused, to find a niche that fit so perfectly.

"Okay," she said, as if her agreement mattered. They both knew it didn't, since she'd basically shanghaied this ride home. "How much longer? A few hours? Half a day?"

Not that anybody would be worrying. She hadn't told her parents when she'd be home, since she'd been hoping to talk Benny into waiting a few extra days so she could stockpile a little more cash.

"Two, maybe three days," Tyler said, dropping the bomb in an easy drawl.

"Two or three…"

"Extra days," he finished with a nod, gathering their breakfast leftovers onto the tray to return to the diner.

"Days," she echoed faintly. She grabbed the remaining

apples and salad from the tray, tucked them into her bag. She'd only budgeted enough for one day's worth of travel food, knowing she'd be well fed as soon as she got home. How the hell was she going to stretch her funds to three days?

Rita did a quick mental count of the cash tucked away in her bag. Still a few hundred shy for the payment on the victrola.

She was so screwed. Pressing her hand to her stomach, she tried to quell the panic. Somehow, some way, she had to salvage this. Because Rita Mae Cole had learned the hard way not to let herself get screwed unless she knew the pleasure was worth the price.

THEY'D BEEN ON THE ROAD awhile and Tyler was still grinning. His plan was brilliant. He'd called a few buddies to spread the word while he'd been waiting for the food. He'd delay enough to keep Rita away from Randy, who was leaving Christmas evening. If Tyler played it right, they'd get home for Christmas Eve without her catching a clue.

So what if it meant he spent a few more days in her company? It wouldn't be a major hardship. He glanced over, his smile dimming a notch at the glum look on her face. Her forehead resting on the window, she stared out like the answer to every question in the world was written on the side of the freeway.

Should he ask what was wrong? He wasn't supposed to care, he reminded himself. She was a big girl, well able to take care of herself. But the dejected droop of her shoulders was really getting to him.

"Hey—"

"What town are we going to?" she interrupted. She didn't look so dejected now, thanks to the slightly manic gleam in her big green eyes. "Do you know about when we'll get there?"

"Um…" He gauged the expression on her face, wondering if she was about to throw a monkey wrench in his plans.

"Chatsworth. We'll be there in an hour, hour and a half, I'd guess. Why?"

She just shrugged, bending over to dig into the huge tote bag she'd plopped at her feet. Resurfacing with a cell phone that looked as if it could run complex algebraic formulas, she sent her fingers flying over the tiny keys.

"What're you doing?"

"Just...I'm not sure," she admitted, her fingers freezing for a second as she stared out the window again. Tyler leaned forward to glance past her, trying to figure out what the hell she was staring at.

Apparently she didn't see it either, because she dove into the bag again. This time she pulled out a thick stack of papers, puffing out her cheeks as she flipped through them. She nodded and tucked them under her thigh, then resumed tapping on the phone.

"Rita?"

"Hmm?" She stopped tapping long enough to glance over. "Oh, I'm just, well, working on a little Christmas project. It's for my parents."

As soon as the words cleared her lush lips, she winced and wrinkled her nose. "Sort of. In a roundabout way."

And those confusing words were all she'd say about it. For the next forty-five minutes, over the Christmas carols belting out of the radio, Tyler peppered Rita with questions.

She was polite. She was even sweet. She texted like a maniac. She scanned the pages, somehow not getting nauseous, which made Tyler a little jealous. He couldn't read in a moving car without tossing his lunch.

But by the time she'd settled down with the papers, a red pen and a blank notebook, he'd gotten no more out of her than when he'd started. When she began humming along to "Silent Night," he gave up.

Thirty minutes later he left the freeway. Taking that as some kind of signal, Rita hit the bag once again, pulling out a cosmetic bag and going to work. In the ten minutes it took Tyler to reach the small bike shop on the far side of a strip mall, she'd transformed her face from naked to sultry.

He told himself he was feeling antsy because he needed to get out and stretch his legs. But since his third leg was stretching quite nicely on its own, he had to cop to self-delusion.

Killing the engine, he kept his gaze on the shop instead of looking at Rita again. "You want to come in?"

"Nah, I've got some things to do still," she said distractedly. "I need to get into my stuff in the back, though. Okay?"

"Sure," he agreed, jumping out of the truck in unseemly haste and hobbling toward the safety of men, bikes and the scent of motor oil.

After twenty minutes of BSing with his buddy, Roy, and a few biker pals, guilt set in. He'd thought Rita would have joined him by now. It was pretty damned cold out there. Telling the guys he'd be back, he headed toward the truck. Within a few feet he could see she wasn't in the cab, so he rounded the bed.

He could barely pick her out in the crowd. Bikers were shoulder to shoulder with what looked like bankers from the S and L on the corner. Mixed in were a few gals with huge hair that he suspected worked at the beauty salon in the mall.

"What the hell…" He stared, slack-jawed, as Rita waved her hand, all game-show hostess like, over the array of vividly colored items spread across the tailgate of his truck.

"What the hell are these?" she clarified, stepping around two blondes to greet him.

Even knowing he was no better than one of Pavlov's pups, Tyler swept his gaze over her face, now pinup-girl exotic. Her hair was still in a ponytail, but she'd done something to make it look all fifties' movie-star flirty. She was still in the same jeans she'd worn earlier, but she'd replaced her red puffy jacket with a black studded leather one.

Tyler's mouth watered.

"These are toys," she said. It took him five seconds and the direction of her pointing finger to remember the question.

"Toys."

"Sex toys."

"I realize they're sex toys. Why are they here? Now? On my truck?" He stared, fixated, at a foot-long, neon-green monstrosity with the head—and face—of a dinosaur.

Her laugh was all it took to rip his attention from the freakish dildo back to her. She ran her tongue over her upper teeth to hide a smirk, he was sure.

"I see you're interested in the T-Sex—the dinosaur of dildos," she explained, sounding like a TV commercial hawking a new model car. "Guaranteed to make your woman roar with pleasure."

"What…"

"What am I doing with them? Selling them, of course." She indicated the little slips of paper she'd tucked underneath each toy. He squinted, seeing she'd not only written up descriptions, but detailed suggestions for ways to use them, along with the asking price.

Tyler was grateful the icy wind was there to cool his cheeks before the heat became apparent.

Didn't matter, though. Rita, probably having a special radar for that kind of thing, laughed.

She leaned forward and gave his cheek a soft pat. The smooth touch of her fingers made him want to grab her wrist and nibble his way up her arm.

"Don't worry, big boy," she purred. "You can have first dibs. I'll even give you a good-driver discount."

The only thing that kept Tyler from grabbing her by that tiny waist, tossing her in the bed of the truck and showing her just exactly *how* good he could drive was the six-and-a-half-foot biker in studded leather who'd tapped her on the shoulder and asked the price of a set of candy-cane-styled nipple rings.

4

"SEX TOYS?"

Rita tried not to giggle as she counted her cash. Tyler had been repeating that same phrase for the past half hour. Over and over and over. You'd think the guy had never seen a plastic rainbow cock ring before.

"Do you have a personal or moral issue with pleasure aids?" she asked, tucking her tongue in her cheek as she noted the sold prices on her inventory list. Woot! She wouldn't starve on the drive home. Not too shabby considering only three of the people she'd texted had shown up. She'd sold more to the guys in the bike shop than anyone else. Maybe that's why Tyler was freaking.

"You said this was for your parents," he accused.

"My parents have sex."

"With toys?"

"How would I know?" Rita set her papers aside and gave him a curious look. "Are you one of those people who think the 'rents don't do the deed? Don't you think your mom gets her happy on from time to time?"

His wince was almost as intense as his glare.

"Don't." He ground out the word. "Do not go there."

Rita giggled. He was so cute when he got all stiff-faced and protective.

"Don't worry, I'm pretty sure I heard rumor of immaculate conception where you were concerned," she consoled. Tyler rolled his eyes but couldn't disguise his grin. She reached over to pat his thigh. She'd intended the gesture to be friendly.

Instead she felt she'd singed her fingers. Quickly pulling her hand back from those rock-hard muscles, she grabbed the inventory list and stared at the blurry words.

A part of her was doing the jump-up-and-down scream, yelling for her to go for it. They had the next few days together, just the two of them all cozied up here in the truck. He was gorgeous and sexy, and if the high school rumor mill held any truth—which was debatable, given how easily her sister had started her own rumor to get even with Tyler for ruining her prom—he was one helluva hot lover. And that had been eight years ago. She would bet he'd improved with age.

Oh man, she was getting turned-on. It was probably because it'd been forever since she'd been with anyone. She knew guys looked at her and automatically thought easy sex. But to Rita, sex just for the sake of getting naked was like an empty gift box under the Christmas tree. Enticing and maybe sparkly fun on the outside, but a mondo huge disappointment in the long run.

And with Tyler?

Somehow, she knew if they got sexy together, she'd want to keep whatever was inside that pretty package for herself. And that it would hurt like crazy when she couldn't.

"Why?" he asked a few dozen miles later.

Ripped from the sappy realization, she started. Had he read her mind?

"Why what?"

"Why are you carting around a box of kink?"

Rita's lips twitched. "I have to say, I'm a little surprised," she mused. "I had no idea you were such a prude."

"The hell I am," he defended, tearing his gaze from the road to glare at her. "I'm all for sex. All kinds, all ways, all places. I could tell you stories that'd…"

Rita bit her lip to keep her smile from turning into a chortle.

"Once upon a time…" she encouraged.

He shot her a long look that was obviously going for irritated. But she saw his lips twitch.

"I'm not a prude," he reiterated.

"But you are a party pooper if you're not going to finish that little story."

"Sex toys. Your parents. Common ground?"

His fingers were now tapping an impatient beat on the steering wheel. Rita thought of the favor she needed to ask. Probably best to stop the teasing right about now, she decided.

"I want to get my parents this fabulous present for Christmas."

"You haven't already got their present?" he said. "Christmas is in five days."

Rita narrowed her eyes. "What are you, the calendar police?"

"Fine. You found the perfect present that you haven't bought yet. Keep going."

Rita poked her bottom lip out. "I don't have quite enough money yet. Which was why I was working the bar. Tips are great this time of year and I'd figured another night would've been all I needed for the final payment."

His wince was worth a thousand apologies. Never one to hold a grudge—after all, she so often screwed things up herself—Rita felt the last vestiges of irritation with Tyler's job-costing kiss fade.

"No biggie," she said, wanting to erase that guilty look from his face. "The gal I was staying with, Shawn? She owns an erotic bookstore. She gave me a whole box of misfit toys as a going-away present."

You had to credit Tyler. He was quick on the uptake. One glance at the inventory in her lap and he said, "So you're selling them on the road to make up the money you lost."

"Exactly." She twisted to pull one knee up on the seat and face him. "But to make it work, I sort of need a favor."

"I'm not demonstrating those damned things for you," he yelped, going pale.

Rita grinned, the image of just how he'd look in that black leather cock ring flashing through her mind. Mmm-mmm good. She shook her head, but still reached over to turn the heater down a little.

"Nothing like that. I just need a quick stop at the next town to get a few Christmas stockings, some holiday ribbon and bows. Maybe some mistletoe. Packaging, you know?"

"Packaging," he repeated faintly.

"Yep." She flipped the inventory over for a blank writing surface and held up her pen. "And if you're willing to be a total sweetie pie, you could give me a rundown of our itinerary. That way I can get the word out, drum up some interest ahead of time."

He opened his mouth as if to answer, then his brow furrowed and he gave her a weird look. His shoulders hunched a little and he gripped the wheel tighter.

"Drum up interest? How?"

"Social networking at its best," she explained. "My phone has apps for Facebook, Twitter and a couple others. Over the years I've met about a million people. I'll tweet the location, the time and a few tasty tidbits. Then, hopefully, there'll be buyers waiting when we get there."

It was a great plan. From the stunned look on Tyler's face, he thought so, too. Or maybe that was horror?

"So what d'ya say?" she asked. "Can I get the itinerary?"

"I, um, have to make some calls first. Check on the guys who wanted me to stop by, see if they still want to talk." He shot her a look so sweet, she got a sugar rush. "I'll hit the next town so you can do some shopping, okay? Make my calls and give you tomorrow's stops at least."

The smile he gave her was little-boy cute, with just a hint of something naughty beneath the surface. It was all Rita could do not to unhook her seat belt and climb into his lap.

"Sure," she said softly, giving him a slow, sexy look from under her lashes. "Whatever you want."

When his eyes narrowed, she ran her tongue along her bottom lip and gave a sigh. Small enough to be cute, but big enough to draw his attention to the ample curves of her chest. Which was covered, unfortunately, in an ancient blue sweater that owed its life to comfort and warmth, not fashion.

No matter. It wasn't as if she was going to dig into the package of sex toys herself. That'd be crazy. He was totally wrong for her. And then there was the fact that her family, who had never gotten over the prom fiasco, would kill her.

Of course, when had she worried what her family thought? Rita glanced at the list of toys she was trying to sell and winced. So she always worried about what her family thought. Which meant that until she knew she could handle whatever came up—or didn't come up—she'd just play with the wrappings.

But, oh, sweet holiday, she was damned sure unwrapping Tyler Ramsey would be one incredible pleasure. And she was definitely woman enough to handle anything he had tucked away in those faded jeans.

The trick would be convincing him. And she'd get right on that, just as soon as she was sure she could afford what doing so would cost her.

DRIVING THROUGH THE SNOW, Tyler gratefully listened to Rita chatter. He'd damn near driven off the road an hour back after getting blasted by a major sexy vibe. But after a few zinging hot seconds, she'd put her come-hither look away and turned on the friendly charm.

He couldn't honestly say he preferred friendly to sexy; he had to admit Rita was appealing either way.

Upbeat and gregarious, she covered topics ranging from what she'd gotten her sisters for Christmas, to who sang a better version of "Santa Baby" and how to build a perfect snowman.

She discussed his bike business, showing a surprising grasp of the bikes themselves and the Harley mystique. She talked about her myriad jobs, ranging from her stint as a restaurant critic to babysitting show dogs. From the sound of it, she'd taken jack-of-all-trades-master-of-none to new levels.

She filled him in on the friends she'd made, the people she'd connected with during her career odyssey, including the fact that she had all of them either on Twitter, Facebook or email. A huge benefit for her toy caper, he had to acknowledge.

The more he listened, the less he knew her. And the more he wanted her.

Which was crazy. Rita was trouble, wasn't she? She was bad news to any guy crazy enough to fall under her green-eyed spell. But the sweet look on her face when she'd described the present she wanted to get her parents was stuck in his brain.

Sure, he still felt justified with his actions back in the bar. He'd wanted to save Benny from making an ass out of himself. But he'd also ruined Rita's Christmas, not only her finances, but her entire homecoming. What kind of jerk was he? It wasn't like Benny wouldn't make an ass of himself anyway, and now that he'd spent some time with Rita, he realized she wasn't the do-him-for-a-ride-home type.

The question was, was he the do-the-girl-his-brother-had-loved type?

Four hours later, Tyler stood before a glass door painted with a snowman in a Santa hat. He shoved it open with as much force as the wind would allow, entered an almost-empty diner and stomped the snow from his feet.

There on the counter next to the doughnut display was Rita's little display of sex toys, all tied in festive ribbons or tucked into jolly red-and-white fuzzy stockings.

Looking like a naughty elf displaying her wares, Rita perched on the red and chrome stool next to the toys. The lights from a seventies' era silver metallic Christmas tree flashed, giving the entire scene a surreal edge.

"Don't you look like quite the grump. Or in keeping with the season, make that Scrooge." She winked, then flicked a quick finger at the fringe of the snow-encrusted scarf he wore. "What's the matter?"

Frustrated on more levels than he'd known he had, Tyler stared into the dancing depths of her dark green eyes. Lush lashes and the exaggerated dark liner gave her the look of a very satisfied, very seductive cat.

A cat that had gotten over any and all skittishness he might have comforted himself by thinking she felt. That's what he got for relaxing his guard. Now he saw her as a woman. A woman who was sweet, funny and totally devoted to her family. One that, damn him, he actually liked.

And he had no one to blame but himself.

"We're stuck." Tyler gave her the news as he threw himself into an empty booth and bounced a fist on the table. "Snow's shut down the freeway until tomorrow."

Eyes widening, Rita glanced past him at the falling snow.

"The state trooper told me the motel up the highway is filled," Tyler added. "He suggested we hunker down here or in the truck."

"Be right back," she murmured.

Tyler shrugged and continued to glare at the fluffy white curse. It was his own fault. He'd just had to take the long, scenic route. If he'd headed straight for Tennessee, they'd have missed the storm and been home tomorrow.

His only consolation was that they'd be spending the night

in the truck. Yes, it'd be cold as hell and miserably uncomfortable. But the combination of discomfort and a semi-public parking lot would insure he kept his hands off Rita's tempting body.

Maybe.

"Good news," she said as she sashayed back over to the booth, two cups of steaming coffee in hand. "The cook, Doris, and I were chatting. She's trading me a Merry Merry Mistletoe stocking of toys in exchange for letting us use the room upstairs."

As always, the mention of Rita's little sideline flipped his switch, tuning his imagination to the many different ways he'd like to feel her come.

And now they had a room? His resistance was down to the dregs. There was no way he'd be able to keep his hands off her if they shared a room.

"Don't worry," she said, patting his hand as if she'd read his thoughts. "It'll only be for one night. Your virtue is safe."

She grinned, wiggled her brows, then added, "Enough."

5

TYLER LUGGED HIS BACKPACK and Rita's tote bag up a rickety flight of dry-rotted wood stairs, squinting against the brightly colored Christmas lights flashing through the snow flurries. Still, when he reached the top step, he hesitated. Could he handle this? A gust of snow hit his face like a fist. Did he have a choice?

Fingers numb in his thick gloves, he pried the door open to find a warm studio apartment that carried the fading scent of baked bread. A pot of coffee sat warming on the hot plate. A really pathetic Charlie Brown Christmas tree listed in the corner, boughs sagging under the weight of the tinsel. And Rita, looking like pure temptation, curled up all cozy and welcoming in a blanket on the floor.

Maybe a night in the truck wouldn't hurt that much?

"Heat, food, a cozy place to crash," Rita said from across the room. "All the comforts of home, huh?"

Tyler grunted. He did a quick inventory. A table, two chairs, a lumpy couch and a couple end tables.

And no bed.

"What's wrong?" she asked softly. So softly he could barely hear the flirtation beneath her teasing tone. "Afraid I'll bite?"

Hell, yeah.

"You're hardly the scary type, sweetheart," he said. Her words were enough to goad him over the threshold, though. "I'm just not big on sharing space."

"Right," she said with an agreeable nod. "Because we've just spent the day in a four-by-five-foot truck cab, and I noticed how totally uncomfortable and out of sorts that made you."

Well, he'd walked right into that one. Tyler wondered if the snow had frozen a few too many brain cells. If it had, his lust should thaw them right out. God, he had to get out of here before he did something crazy. Like give in to not only his current desire, but the other ten years of built-up passion that'd been trying to explode ever since he'd tasted Rita in that damned bar.

"Is it the sex toys?" she asked when he couldn't find the right words.

Tyler's jaw dropped. And, of course, his gaze flew to the box of colorful toys and wrapping, which looked like one of Santa's really kinky elves had been hard at work. Rita was sitting was sitting cross-legged now, gift wrapping the toys. His mouth watered as his attention snagged on a bottle of peppermint-flavored body oil.

"Why would the toys be a problem?" he asked, as if the constant barrage of sexual images they inspired wasn't causing his body a moment's stress. "We already had this talk, didn't we? I'm not a prude."

Just because he was too much of a gentleman to jump her body didn't make him uptight, dammit. It made him…what? Crazy? Frustrated? Teetering on hornily insane?

"Look, the toys aren't a problem," he told her, stuffing his hands in the front pocket of his jeans to disguise how much of a nonproblem they were. "I just don't think it's a good idea for the two of us to be here, sharing a room. You're a great gal and I really like you," he added, a little surprised to realize just how true that was. "But I don't want to make you uncomfortable, or to give you the wrong idea."

There. He'd sounded both reasonable and convincing. Determined, yet friendly. Tyler dropped into a chair, relieved. Not bad for a guy sporting a half-frozen hard-on.

Head tilted to one side, Rita listened attentively. When he wound down, she finished tying a pair of fur-lined handcuffs with a bright red velvet ribbon, then set them aside.

"The wrong idea?"

"You know, like…"

"Like something could happen between us?"

"Exactly." Tyler pointed a finger at her as if she'd just scored a point, then realized he'd agreed with her. "No. I mean, I'm not assuming something would happen just because we're together in a room."

"Really?" She slowly rose to her feet, her fluffy blue sweater and baggy, cuffed jeans sexier than any form of black lace. "You don't think all that time together in close quarters has us thinking crazy thoughts about each other?"

He nodded, mesmerized by the sight of her bare feet, with their candy-cane-striped toenails.

"Or maybe it's the sex toys. You know, constant exposure to the kink is wearing down our resistance." She gave a little shrug, her body brushing against his as she stepped in front of him.

"I don't think it's any of that, though. I think it's us. There's something hot between us." She stood so close now he could feel the whisper of air as her lips moved inches from his. "I think I'd like to see what it is."

Her palm warmed his thigh, leaving tingles as it slid upward. His eyes fogged. She gracefully lowered herself between his knees. He damned near whimpered at the sight of her, looking like some good-ol'-boy fantasy.

"Don't you think it could be a mistake?" he asked, his voice so husky he was surprised he could get the words out.

Her smile should have been declared illegal. Wicked and bright, it lit up her eyes and made his brain sputter. She arched one dark brow, then slid a whisper-soft hint of a kiss over his lips.

Pulling back, she tilted her head and traced a finger along the crease of his thigh, heading toward his bulging zipper.

"If you like, we can always blame it on the mistletoe."

"Oh, no. I'm keeping all the blame, or credit, for myself," Tyler declared.

He didn't give himself time to find his sanity. Instead he tunneled his hands through the silky mass of her hair and tilted her head back, finally giving in to the endless craving that'd been driving him crazy.

THIS WAS WHY SHE WAS always in trouble, Rita realized as Tyler's tongue plunged between her lips. She saw something that looked fun. She couldn't resist trying it out, even though she knew it wasn't right for her. She got caught up in the experience. Then when she ignored all the warning signals and it exploded in her face, she was always devastated and shocked.

But, at this moment, she didn't care. Tyler's lips were the stuff of magic. Soft and hard at the same time, they coaxed hers into a sweet dance. His vivid blue eyes held hers captive, making the kiss all the sexier for that extra intimacy.

Still on her knees, Rita shifted. Sliding her hands up his thighs, she felt his breath catch. Heat surged, igniting intense need deep in her belly. She wanted to touch him, to feel him. To taste him—all of him.

She couldn't believe she was this turned-on by the simple touch of his mouth on hers and his hands in her hair. God, once he hit the erogenous zones, she'd explode fully clothed.

Instead of tracing the hard length stretching his zipper, she forced herself to draw out her excitement by sliding her hands up the rippling planes of his chest.

He moaned lightly as she curled her nails into the delicious muscles of his shoulders. Then, as if that was the signal he'd been waiting for, the kiss went from sweet to erotic in one swift thrust of his tongue.

She hadn't known how afraid she'd been that he'd turn her away until he didn't. Or how much she'd wanted him until he'd taken her mouth with a passion she knew was real. As his tongue swept over hers, his teeth skimming her lower lip to take the kiss even deeper, she forgot every reason why this could be wrong and gave in to all the reasons it was right.

Tyler. Finally. She'd wanted him forever. She'd thought of nothing but his kiss since he'd first brushed his lips over hers in the bar. And now she could touch him, taste him. Be with him. It was like a dream come true.

He shifted. Between one breath and the next, they were both flat on the floor, his body poised over hers, one hand cradling the back of her head. All without taking his lips from her mouth.

Rita had to appreciate a man with that kind of talent.

To show that appreciation, she skimmed her hands down his back and tugged his shirt free of his jeans.

"Mmm," she moaned as she finally got her hands on the warm, hard flesh of his abs. "You have one fine body."

"Ditto," he breathed as he trailed his fingers over the aching heaviness of her breast, then down her waist. Too fast, she wanted to say. She bit back the words. At this rate, she'd be begging before he'd dropped his jeans.

And if there was any begging in this room, it was damned sure going to be mutual.

With that in mind, when he reached for her sweater, she gently batted his hand away.

"This is like a dream come true," she told him, squirming a little. As she moved his eyes went dark and blurry. His breath seemed to stutter in his chest. And best of all? His dick pressed even harder against her thigh.

Before she could give in to the delight of being seduced, she wiggled out from under him. Tyler rolled to his back, watching her with a sexy half smile that challenged her to drive him crazy.

A challenge she was more than happy to take.

Rita reached back to slide the elastic band from her hair, shaking her head so the tresses fell in wild abandon around her face.

She reached down, hooking her fingers on the hem of her sweater, and slowly, inch by inch, started sliding it up her torso.

"You know what I love best about sex?" she asked him, wanting to see if she could break his concentration.

"Everything?" he said absently, his eyes never leaving her body.

"Exactly." Pleased, she finished pulling the sweater off to reward them both. Tossing it aside, she shifted to her knees, then curved her hands over her own waist. In a slow, teasing move she trailed her fingers up her sides, pausing briefly to cup her breasts as if offering them up for Tyler's delight.

His eyes narrowed, and his breath puffed out in appreciation. Her own eyes at half-mast, she scraped her fingernails over her hard nipples where they were trying to break through the lace of her bra. Then, before she could get carried away, she finished the move by tracing her hands up her throat and through her hair, stretching her arms overhead in supplication.

"Sex, when it's done right, is incredible," she said. "It's honest and pure and real. It's all about sharing what's inside, while feeling incredible outside. So...will we do it right?"

She waited, a part of her sure he'd pull away. Instead he tugged off his shirt, then gave her a smile that was so warm, so sweet that her heart melted.

"Why don't I show you," he offered, reaching out to cup his own hands over her breasts. While his fingers worked magic,

Rita hurried the process along by slipping off her jeans and panties, then kneeling over him clad in just her black lace bra.

One hand never leaving her nipples, he used the other to release the catch of her bra before scooping lower to trace the tidy patch of wet curls between her legs.

Leaning back, Rita spread her legs wide to give him better access. One of his hands worked the pouty pink tips of her lush breasts, the other caressed the glistening bud of her desire.

Rita was going to go crazy if he didn't put his finger, his dick—hell, anything—inside her soon.

"More," she demanded breathlessly.

"Make me," he ordered.

Grinning at the command, she took him at his word. Pressing both hands against his chest, she pushed him flat on the floor.

Rita licked and nibbled her way across his glorious chest then down the firm planes of his belly. Obviously too impatient to wait, he tugged his belt open, unsnapped, unzipped and shoved his jeans off. Before she could ask, he held up a foil packet.

With a wink, she took both it and the long, hard length of his dick in hand. Before she sheathed him, she swirled her tongue around the velvet head, making him groan.

"Sit up," she told him. He raised a brow but didn't question the order. He shifted upright, his abs rippling at the move, so his back was against the couch.

Rita straddled him.

Loving the power, the intensity the position afforded her, she slowly, ever so slowly, impaled herself on his rigid shaft. With a moan, she arched her back. Eyes closed, she whimpered as he took the hint, his tongue and fingers working her nipples while she locked her legs behind his waist.

Body to body, face-to-face, eye to eye, they rode the building pleasure higher and higher. The intensity climbed, winding tighter. Her breath came in gasps now as Rita tried to hold out, to hold back the crashing waves of desire.

Tyler shifted his hands from her breasts to grip her hips, guiding her up and down, in and out. Faster and faster. The climax was there, just beyond her reach. With every plunge, she added a little undulation, trying to reach it. Tyler's head fell back against the couch, his eyes closed. His fingers bit into her flesh.

One more thrust was all it took. Rita cried out with the power of her orgasm. Her body shook and her breath caught tight in her chest as she tried to extract every drop of delight from the moment.

Tyler's body stiffened, his hips lifting off the floor as he exploded in his own climax. Rita wrapped her thighs tighter around his hips, her feet locked behind his back as she collapsed against his chest.

They stayed like that for what felt like hours. Rita's breath calmed, and her brain started to clear as she listened to Tyler's heart pound against her ear.

"Now *that*," he breathed, running his hand over her hair, "is what I love about sex."

6

WHILE HER BODY WAS FEELING pretty awesome, Rita still watched the familiar Virginia roads flying by with mixed emotions.

She should be on top of the world. She'd spent the past two nights with a sexy, amazingly inventive lover whom she'd crushed on for years. She'd earned enough money selling toys to pay off the victrola and get her sisters a few more things as well.

So why was she bumming?

She watched an exit sign fly by, recalling that her parents had performed in a center right down that road. Her sisters had sung a duet. And Rita? As usual, she of no talent was out front, handing out flyers and selling CDs. But hey, she recalled with bitter glee, she'd sold the hell out of those CDs.

"What's wrong?" Tyler's question pulled her from her odd reverie.

Rita's gaze flew to his. How did she explain years of doubts to a man who'd never had one? As usual, when faced with sharing her failings, Rita sidestepped right into flirtation.

"Wrong?" she repeated, making the word sound like a naughty proposition. "I'm loose, limber and satisfied. Sweetie, you didn't do anything wrong."

Tyler's grin flashed, but faded just as fast.

"You're still upset," he insisted. "Why?"

Rita wrinkled her nose. "What're you? Mr. Introspection? Did you want to share our emotions? Maybe talk about our future?"

"Maybe we could chat about genital warts or prostate exams instead." He glanced over with a smile. One of those special smiles that could melt her heart and turn her insides to goo.

"Even that'd be more interesting than what's mucking around in my head."

He gave her a quick look. Those gorgeous blue eyes said he was concerned, he cared, and he wanted to make her feel good.

Rita's heart danced along with the holiday song ringing through the truck's speakers.

"C'mon, Rita. Aren't we more than hot, wild sex? What's wrong?"

Yes, they were more than sex. Which was a little scary. "Nothing, really. We used to live in this area. Just for a few months."

"That's it? A few months?"

"You know we moved a lot before my parents settled in Ponder Hill, right?"

"Sure."

"It wasn't bad, really. I mean, we met a ton of people, saw most of the country. I can even credit selling all those sex toys to that." She gave a little smile. "At least half of the people on my social networks that showed up to buy goodies were people I'd met way back when."

"And you kept in touch all these years?"

"Of course. I like people."

From the look on Tyler's face, that was a concept he just didn't get.

"Don't you keep in touch with old friends? Like Benny. You were hanging out with him, right?"

Tyler gave a weird grimace, then shrugged. "Not much. I'd rather spend time on the bikes, working and trying to drum up more business, than sit around talking about days gone by."

She wrinkled her nose. "If you stay in touch, you'd be talking about today, not yesterday."

His expression clearly said he didn't find any more appeal in that than the idea of rehashing his wild teen years. Baffled, Rita shifted her knee up on the bench seat to fully face him.

"You know, if you bothered to keep up, some of those people might help you build your business," she pointed out.

"How?" he challenged with a doubtful laugh.

"They'd remember your name when they want a bike. They'd recommend you to friends." She could see that didn't impress him much, so she pushed harder. "Someone might mention you on a radio show. Or be willing to swap a magazine ad in exchange for a bike tune-up. Remember that gal who was so obsessed with photography back in school?"

"Millie something? Mary? No, Megan, right?"

"Megan Witting," Rita confirmed with a snap of her fingers. "She stuck with the photography. Now she does shoots for all these big national magazines. If you were still in touch, she might have used your bikes in that *GQ* layout she did last year, instead of whatever local yahoo she used."

"Yeah, right."

"Seriously, it happens. I introduced this graphic artist to my boss a few years back when I was working at a bakery. This was in my wannabe-a-pastry-chef days. Not only did the guy design her logo, he ended up doing some great cake designs for her. Then they got married and have their very own baby bump happening."

She spent the next thirty miles regaling him with stories of the power of networking.

Finally, he threw up one hand and laughed. "Fine, fine.

You've convinced me. Social networking isn't a waste of time and remembering people's names is a worthy skill."

Chuckling, Rita gave a decisive nod. "Exactly. And now that you're convinced, I'll draw you up your very own plan." She grabbed a pad of paper and started making notes. "This'll mean you don't ever have to drive two days to deliver a bike again. People will come to you, instead. I'll bet your business picks up at least fifteen percent by summer."

"What? No peace-on-earth promises, too?"

"Give me a few years," she vowed, warmed by his teasing tone. But even more by his absolute faith. Nobody had ever believed in her like this.

"None of this put that sad look in your eyes," Tyler insisted after a few minutes.

Surprised at the return to his original question, Rita answered before she could censor herself. "No, that's just the familiar weight of failure bumming me out."

"WHAT?" TYLER COULDN'T keep the shock from his voice. What the hell was she talking about? "How can you think you're a failure?"

"Well, I'm hardly a success."

He had to force himself to turn his attention back to the road.

"It's not like there are only two choices," he smiled.

"Aren't there?"

He frowned, needing to think that one through.

"No," he insisted. "Success is faceted. Failure is black-and-white."

"I just got fired from my fallback job, the one I always turn to when I fail at yet another career," she told him. "Which is pretty black in my books."

Figuring it best not to point out his part in that job failure, Tyler shook his head. "That's because you keep trying to do the wrong things. But the fact that you keep trying proves you aren't a failure."

"Wrong things?" she repeated, ignoring the rest of his words.

"Yeah. You've already got all you need for the perfect career. You just haven't pulled it together yet."

Looking at him as if he was crazy, Rita shook her head. "What the hell are you talking about?"

"Social networking. Building relationships. Promoting businesses and people. All that stuff you've been lecturing me on. Just look at your notes. You've written three pages of plans for my business already. Do you have any idea how much consultants charge for that kind of thing?"

Tyler laughed at the shock on Rita's face.

"You're a natural," he assured her. "You actually like people and understand how to build friendships, relationships. I've gone to a couple of those promotion seminars they hold at the business center. Those guys talk about networking, but it's just talk. You, on the other hand, really get what the give and take are all about."

Her silence started to make him nervous.

"What?" he prodded. "You don't think it'd work?"

"I've never considered it until just now," she mumbled.

Puzzled at her frown, Tyler reached over to give her hand a squeeze. He didn't understand how a woman as confident and amazing as Rita could doubt her skills.

"Just think it over," he urged her. Not that he planned to give up. Not now that he'd found an idea that might keep her in Ponder Hill. If she ran with it, she could build a successful business right there with him.

Tyler liked that idea. The possibility of building something together. Enough time to see if what was flaming between them was solid enough to last.

Except for one tiny problem.

Randy.

Randy, who not only blamed Rita for all his love life woes, but who regularly brought up the evils of the Cole sisters, adding Alison's treatment of Tyler to his list. A list Tyler had always supported.

He'd been an idiot to judge Rita as he had.

Time to call home and start laying the groundwork toward the Cole girls' redemption.

Because one way or another, he planned to keep Rita Mae as his very own Christmas gift.

7

"THIS WAS A GREAT IDEA," Tyler murmured against the rich fragrance of Rita's hair. "I'm glad the snow forced us to stop early."

Maybe *forced* was the wrong word. He'd seen a few flurries and immediately cited driving dangers, finding the closest hotel and checking them in before dinnertime. Sure, wild roadside lovemaking was great, but he'd wanted a soft bed. A hot shower. And plenty of room to try out the few toys Rita had left.

Tyler didn't know when he'd felt this incredible. With Rita, he didn't have anything to prove. She didn't expect anything from him except that he be himself.

He tightened his arm around her waist and gave a deep sigh.

"S'good?" she murmured sleepily, her breath a warm caress against his skin.

"S'great," he clarified. And it was. He felt he'd finally found that last piece of the puzzle, the one he hadn't even realized he was missing. He had a good life. But with Rita in it, it would be amazing.

The job he loved was going to get even better, thanks to

Rita. His free time was going to be filled with laughter and great sex, thanks to Rita. And his future?

The only problem with planning a future was Randy. Tyler thought about his call home the day before while Rita was selling her toys. He'd tried to broach the subject of getting over exes and the craziness of teenage love, but a recently dumped Randy had launched a rant about the fickleness of women and their lack of heart.

Not the opening Tyler wanted for his suggestion of a special guest for Christmas dinner. And as much as he wanted to tell his brother to grow up, a lifetime of protecting the kid was hard to overcome.

But he was a smart guy. He'd find a way to fix it so Randy got over himself, their mom wasn't upset about her boys fighting, and Tyler got to keep Rita.

Somehow.

"I want to see you in Ponder Hill," he said, figuring tiptoeing into the subject was better than diving.

She tilted her head back, her eyes a pool of sleepy sensuality, and gave him a smile that made his heart sing. "I have to spend Christmas with my family, but I'm sure I can sneak out for a little mistletoe action."

Muscles he hadn't even realized he'd tensed relaxed. She'd so easily accepted that they'd continue to see each other. He was more relived than he wanted to admit. With his free hand, Tyler tucked a stray lock of black hair behind her ear, loving the silky texture.

"I'll be with mine, too." He hesitated. He knew what he wanted to say. Despite the opening, he just wasn't sure how to put it into words, though.

"You know," she said slowly, her fingers tracing a concentrated pattern on his chest, "my family might not be too excited about our dating at first."

"Huh?"

"Prom. You and Alison. Knocked up rumors."

He grimaced.

"But hey," she said quickly. "I'm sure they'll get over it. I mean, it'd be crazy to hold a grudge over a little teenage high jinks, right?"

"High jinks?" He didn't expect Rita to feel guilty for her sister's actions, but…high jinks? "She told the entire school I got her pregnant."

"Well, she was upset."

Her smile faded when she saw the look on his face.

"Kinda like Randy was upset when you dumped him," Tyler shot back. As soon as the words were out, he wanted to take them back.

Rita frowned.

"Dumped? It was hardly that dramatic."

"Are you kidding? He still hasn't gotten over you breaking his heart."

"Breaking his heart?" Rita looked genuinely puzzled. "No way. We only dated a few weeks. It wasn't like it was a grand passion—we never did more than swap a few kisses."

"Is that your criterion for love? How far you go with a guy?" And how pathetic was he when his heart leaped up to do a little victory dance at the fact that their naked exchanges must put him pretty high on the emotional charts.

"I'd say it's a pretty good criterion, wouldn't you?" she teased, obviously trying to lighten the mood. "It takes a strong emotional connection to make the sex incredible. And why waste time on anything less than incredible?"

All his worries melted away.

"Of course, incredible's going to be interesting when my family finds out," Rita said with a little grimace.

"You think *you'll* have a hard time? How do you think it's going to be for me? I'm bringing home one of the Cole girls. And the wildest one, at that."

"The wildest…"

He barely heard Rita's whispered words.

"Randy's got such a major grudge against you, I even went with Benny to that bar to keep you from…"

Tyler's mouth was about two seconds ahead of his brain. By the time the mental warning flashed, it was too late.

Rita pulled back.

"From what?" Her eyes narrowed. "To keep me, the wild Cole sister, away from your brother? Is that why you slept with me? A distraction so I wouldn't go after Randy when we got home?"

"Bad word choice." He gave her his most charming smile. His brain was still stumbling behind, though, and he couldn't think of a good excuse, so he used the fallback option.

Running the palm of his hand along the silky smooth warmth of her hip, he leaned closer to brush his lips over hers.

She hissed. Tyler pulled back fast. From the look in her eyes, she wouldn't hesitate to bite.

RITA FELT SO EMOTIONALLY battered it actually hurt to move. But she'd be damned if she'd lie there bare-assed naked with someone who thought so little of her.

Throwing off the covers, she leaped from the warm bed, suddenly feeling exposed. She grabbed her sweater, pulling it on without bothering with a bra.

"C'mon, sweetheart. Don't be this way." He had the nerve to sound all innocent, like he hadn't just done the emotional equivalent of telling a kid there was no such thing as Santa Claus.

"You hit on me in the bar to piss Benny off," she accused him as realization hit her like a brick wall. Shards of pain sliced through her, making it hard to catch her breath enough to speak. "You were trying to blow my ride home."

That sexy, multiple orgasm glow left his face and it hardened into stiff, unreadable lines. But Tyler didn't say a word.

"You went along with giving me a ride home to keep an

eye on me, didn't you?" He still kept silent, but the answer was clear in his eyes.

"You're making it sound ugly and premeditated, like I was trying to hurt you," he finally said.

Feeling more naked than ever, Rita glanced around the room in search of her jeans. Grabbing her panties, she had them halfway up her thighs when a thought hit her.

"You didn't have any stops to make, did you?" Her breath lodged painfully in her chest, and she had to swallow before continuing. "You made that up to drag the trip out. To give your brother time to get away before I got home."

"Look, you're turning this into a bigger deal than it really is," he protested.

"Do you deny it?" she asked, hoping like crazy he would. Even if it was a lie, she wanted to hear the words.

But Tyler Ramsey never backed down from a fight. Instead he shifted into a sitting position, leaning against the headboard and slapping his arms across his chest.

"I don't deny I was looking out for my family. That's what I do. It had nothing to do with you, really."

Her jeans on now, Rita almost zipped up her fingers as they fumbled in shock at his words. "Nothing to do with me?"

"Look, you're stronger than Randy. You don't get what it's like to fail. To carry a torch, to wish for someone who's way out of your league."

Wasn't her entire life a series of failures? The biggest one lying there naked right now? And she wasn't even talking about the pathetic torch she'd carried for him all these years. Unwilling to let him see her tears, she started packing.

"What're you doing?"

"What's it look like I'm doing?" Hurt fueling her movements, Rita tossed her belongings, willy-nilly, into her tote bag.

"Get real," Tyler chided in that "I'm a man so I can see you're acting ridiculous" tone that made her want to stop tossing things in her bag and aim it at his head instead. "What're you going to do? Sleep in the truck?"

The truck? Sleep? So mad she could barely connect one thought to another, Rita glared. But she didn't slow her packing.

"Don't blow this out of proportion," he ordered.

She wouldn't be surprised if her head exploded. Damned if she shouldn't have stuck with admiring the pretty packaging. An empty box would have been so much better than this miserable mess she'd so gleefully unwrapped.

Rita slung her bag over her shoulder and grabbed her purse, then headed for the door.

"Where the hell are you going?" he demanded.

Hand on the doorknob, Rita stopped. She turned to face him, staring through tear-filled eyes. All sexy and still love-mussed, Tyler stood, hands fisted on hips covered with the draped bedsheet.

"I'm going home," she told him. "You can drop my stuff at my parents'. Or at Benny's. Or wherever."

"Don't be…" Finally catching a clue, Tyler bit off the rest of his admonishment with a quick shake of his head. "Look, you're pissed. I get that. I screwed up, got stuck in the past. Don't let that ruin this."

Ruin what? What the hell was *this,* other than a lie on his part and pure wishful thinking on hers? How stupid was she to actually believe Tyler might see more in her than a sexy body and a pretty face.

"You know what, you're right," she forced herself to admit, although she'd much rather be able to call him an all-around liar. "I did hurt Randy. When I was seventeen. I was careless and selfish. And just as responsible for my actions as you were with Alison."

He frowned. Whether at her confession or the hurt she knew was probably showing on her face, Rita wasn't sure.

"But you, Tyler? You broke my heart on purpose."

"The hell I did." He scowled now and wrapped his sheet tighter. Like she was going to, what? Dive in and get her revenge on his bare boy parts?

"You kissed me in the bar. Why?"

Anger flashed bright in his eyes and he opened his mouth. Then shut it.

God. Even though she'd suspected, confirmation still hurt like crazy. But all she had left was her pride.

So Rita nodded, smirking through the pain. "Exactly."

She yanked the door open, then stopped. Necessity as much as habit had her posing, hip shot out with a sexy toss of her hair as she looked back.

Calling on every ounce of pride she had, Rita lifted her chin and hid the pain ripping through her heart.

With a smile she hoped he saw in his dreams for years to come, she tossed a "Merry freaking Christmas" over her shoulder, then waltzed out.

8

"TYLER MICHAEL RAMSEY, what's wrong with you?"

Tyler winced, slowly lowering the milk carton from his mouth to see his mom glaring from the doorway.

"I'm home," he said, offering up his most charming smile instead of an excuse. Excuses never mattered with Elizabeth Ramsey. A petite, dark-haired firecracker, the woman saw through bullshit like she had X-ray vision or something.

"And you decided to come over to my place for a refresher course in table manners?"

"Well, you have food." He lifted his other hand to show the huge, glittery green, tree-shaped sugar cookie he'd been washing down.

"Put that away," she ordered with a roll of her eyes. "If you want to eat, you'll eat real food."

Pretending that hadn't been his goal all along, Tyler put the cookie on the counter and poured the rest of the milk into the glass his mom handed him. He filled her in on his trip, sans mention of Rita, as he watched her whip up her special blueberry pancakes.

"Where'd Randy go?" he asked as she set the first few in front of him along with the syrup. "He was in a mood when I called, but he wouldn't say why."

"Tyler, you have to stop worrying about your brother. Randy's a big boy. He doesn't need you riding to his rescue." She flipped two more pancakes onto his plate and followed up with a gentle swat to the back of his head. "He especially doesn't need you doing anything stupid like getting into yet another bar fight, beating up some poor guy or doing anything else that makes the ladies I lunch with whisper in outrage."

"I don't—"

"Three months ago, Randy was home for summer break and some bruiser cut him off. What'd you do?" Elizabeth went back to the stove, tossing a glare at Tyler. "You went to the guy's work and called him out on it."

"He dented Randy's car," Tyler defended around a mouthful of rich blueberry pancake.

"You punched him in the church parking lot where he was doing yardwork."

Tyler winced.

"And then there was the time you wanted to drive to Nashville to accost his philosophy teacher for giving him a C."

"Randy said—"

"Or the time you wanted to go after the boy who got the job at the supermarket instead of Randy. You glared at that child every time he bagged my vegetables."

"He bruised the eggplant."

"Tyler."

He gave a bad-tempered shrug and stabbed his fork into his pancake. Wasn't it bad enough he'd blown things with Rita over his brother? Now he was getting a lecture for it.

"Is this going to go on much longer?" Tyler asked, aggrieved. "If so, I need more pancakes."

All it took was a single arched brow for Tyler to offer his plate, along with a "Please."

"It could go on all day, now couldn't it? The point is, you have to stop jumping to Randy's defense. He's not a skinny, helpless little kid any longer."

"So you're saying I should just let Randy get hurt?"

"I'm saying that the things you think are a big deal usually aren't."

Appetite gone, Tyler stared at the fresh stack of blueberry goodness on his plate.

"But—"

"Tyler, do you want to live your life or live Randy's?"

His sigh was worthy of his ten-year-old self, which was how old he'd been the first time he'd heard that question.

And finally, eighteen years later, he got the message.

A faint hope glimmered in his heart. Tracing a pattern in the syrup with his fork, he stared at his plate for a few moments, wondering if he was crazy.

Then he realized it didn't matter. Crazy or not, he had to try. He needed Rita.

"Just so ya know," he told his mom as he got up to carry his plate to the sink, "I'm probably bringing someone home for Christmas dessert."

Elizabeth's swift intake of breath showed she knew the significance. But in her usual, unflappable way, she tilted her head and only asked, "Anyone I know?"

"Rita Cole," he said, his jaw jutting out as he waited.

Her smile melted away his last doubt. "Rita Mae? Oh, how is she doing? I hear from her mama all the stories of her travels and can't wait to see her again. What a fun girl she was. And—" she stopped gushing to give her eldest son a shrewd look "—perfect, I think. For you, that is."

"You and Rita's mom are on speaking terms?"

Elizabeth smiled, amused. "After your prom, I felt it necessary to meet the possible mother of my future grandchild."

"Shit."

She laughed, patting his hand in that indulgent mom way. "Despite that, Amanda and I have become good friends over the years. She even helps out every once in a while at the antiques store."

A lightbulb shaped like a peace offering flashed in Tyler's head.

"Rita is perfect," he acknowledged. "But I screwed up a little. Will you help me fix things?"

THERE WAS NO PLACE LIKE home on Christmas Eve. Rita sighed, cupping her hands around the steaming cup of cocoa, and breathed in the delicious comfort of her mom's favorite cure-all.

Just like the cocoa meant home, so did the music playing a gentle holiday medley in the background. All Rita's life there had been music. Always. Other than their devotion to each other and their daughters, Eric and Amanda's main focus in life was music. After years of performing, they were now happy to teach and pass their love on to others.

Which was why Rita had wanted to give them music for Christmas. Special music. Music that would not only show how much she'd appreciated them, but prove that they no longer had to worry, stress or wonder where they'd gone wrong with her.

And what'd she spent the money on? A plane ticket home. Why? Because she'd been so freaking stupid.

So again this year, her holiday offerings would take on the equivalent of a grade-schooler with some glitter and tasty paste.

"Rita?"

"In here, Mom."

Amanda Cole came into the room, a smaller, leaner version of her daughter. She shot Rita one quick, encompassing glance, then flipped the tree lights on so the eve-darkened room was drenched in celebratory color.

"Making Christmas wishes?" her mother asked with a smile as she settled next to Rita on the couch.

"I'm not sure what I'd wish for," Rita said, since murder and dismemberment seemed so unholidaylike.

"What's the matter, sweetie?"

Rita started to offer up one of her typical lines of BS. Some "can't worry Mom at the holidays" fluff that would pacify her worries and leave Rita to be miserable in private.

But the steady look in her mother's green eyes, their shape and intensity so like her own, froze the words in Rita's throat.

"I think I'm in…"

She couldn't get the words out.

"In trouble?" her mom offered hesitantly.

Rita shook her head.

Amanda sat on the arm of the sofa to get a better look at her daughter's face in the flashing colors of the tree lights. A quick study, a widening of her own eyes, then she puffed out a breath.

"In…love?"

A hot sting burned Rita's eyelids. She bit her lip to keep from letting the burn turn to actual tears.

"It sucks," she declared.

"Oh, sweetie." The wealth of love, understanding and empathy in those simple words was too much for Rita. Heated misery poured down her cheeks as her mother enfolded her in soft arms, the familiar scent of Chanel as comforting as the hug.

"Who is he?" Amanda asked as the crying jag wore down.

Rita winced. For an entire second, she debated not telling. After all, she and Tyler were through. But she'd never been able to lie to her mom. Sidestep? Yes. Direct lie? Never.

"Tyler Ramsey," she mumbled against her mom's shoulder.

Silence. Then, "Well, your daddy's got a strong heart. He'll bounce back from the shock fast enough."

Rita gasped, making her mother laugh and give her another hug.

"Don't worry, sweetie."

In spurts and jags, Rita filled her mom in on the ride home, the hopes she'd let herself have, then the heartbreak she'd felt when she'd realized that Tyler could never see past the wild side of her enough to really care.

Anger drying her tears, she punched the pillow she'd been hugging. "It was all some stupid game to him. A setup to make sure I didn't get in the way of his family holiday and give his brother ideas again."

"Now that doesn't sound right." At Rita's look, Amanda shrugged. "I'm not saying he didn't set out to cause a ruckus. That sounds like Tyler. That boy never engages his brain before he jumps into gear. But why would he give you a ride home if he was that malicious, Rita Mae? Maybe he was worried about his brother, but that's habit. Tyler had to step into the role of head of that family awfully young and he takes the job seriously."

Frowning, Rita threaded her fingers through the fringe on the pillow. "I thought you didn't like him. You and Dad were so mad at him for what he did to Alison."

"Well, you have to admit, Alison had a little hand in what happened, too," Amanda said with a laugh. "She just had to get her revenge. In addition to being smart, talented and clever, all my girls know how to take care of themselves."

All. That included her. Rita's heart melted. That simple statement, not even directed at her, made her realize that maybe some of her freaking out that her parents didn't have faith in her wasn't justified.

"Was he out of line with you, Rita Mae?"

"No," Rita said immediately. "Tyler was never disrespectful. He acted like I was this combination of Bettie Page, Madonna and that really smart money chick who has a show on TV. He actually thinks more of me than I do of myself."

"How so?"

Rita leaned back so she could watch her mother's face as

she told her about Tyler's career suggestions and all the ideas he'd prompted her to come up with. Then, shoulders knotted, she waited.

"And what do you think about this?"

Rita winced, not wanting to commit one way or another until she knew if her mom approved or not.

Amanda arched her brow. Rita sucked in a deep breath, then puffed it out.

"I'll admit, it's nothing I ever dreamed of doing. And it's not fancy or special or one of those great careers you and Dad would be proud to brag about." Then she added with a shrug, "But I think I'd be good at it, Mom. I think I could make it a success."

"First and foremost, if it makes you happy, isn't it a dream career?" Amanda asked. "Darling, the only way you could disappoint us is if you gave up. On your dreams, or on yourself. You're the only one judging yourself, not us. But I'll save that lecture for later. When your dad's here to enjoy it."

The assurance didn't wipe away all of Rita's doubts or confidence issues. But it did make her realize just how much those issues were of her own making. With a watery smile, she wiped away the tears dripping off her chin and wished she'd stop leaking.

Then with a deep breath, she sucked in her courage, gave her mom a quick hug and slid off the couch.

"Where're you going?" her mom asked.

"I figured out what I want for Christmas," Rita declared. "Now I just have to go get him."

"That's my girl," Amanda declared. "I'm heading over to drop gifts at the Burgoons'. Call if you need me."

Rita hadn't done more than repair her makeup and fluff her hair when the doorbell rang. She hurried to open it, wanting to send the visitors on their way so she could go after her man.

But surprise, surprise. Like a special delivery from Santa, Tyler stood there on the front porch, a huge box in his arms and a charming smile on his face. She could see the nerves in his sexy blue eyes, though.

"Hey, Rita," he greeted. "Wanna ask me in before the snow messes up this pretty present?"

Shocked, she stepped aside so he could cross over and put the big box on the dining table.

Sure, she'd been all set to chase him down, but now that he was here, looking so gorgeous and expectant, she had no clue what to say. So she cocked her hip to one side, crossed her arms under her breasts and lifted her chin.

"I, um, brought this," he said, pointing at the box.

"For me?" she asked, not really caring but too anxious to ask why he was really there. "What is it?"

"This?" Tyler looked over at the festively wrapped gift, complete with ribbon, bells and a sprig of holly, and shrugged. "It's an apology, a bribe or a peace offering. Whichever's necessary."

"All of that in one box?" Rita stepped closer to poke at the large, heavy package. "Can I open it?"

"It's not really for you," he said with a sheepish smile.

"You brought me an apology, bribe and offering that belongs to someone else?"

Now that she was closer, Rita could see the doubt in those sexy blue eyes as he shoved his hands in the front pockets of his jeans.

"It's your victrola," he said in a hushed tone. "It's my fault you spent your money on a plane ticket. I guess you haven't kept up much on town happenings to know my mom bought the antiques store about five years ago. She told me you'd called the store to say you couldn't make the last payment so I made it for you."

"You did?" She forced herself to consider reality this time, not just what she wished to see. "Why? Out of guilt?"

"Yes. No." Tyler shoved a hand through his hair and gave her a frustrated look. "I mean, I did feel guilty about being such a jerk, and about screwing up your Christmas. But that's not why I did it. I know how much it meant to you. How hard you'd worked for it. I just wanted..."

He shrugged, then gave her a look so heart-meltingly sweet her knees went soggy. "I just wanted everyone to see how wonderful you were. How sweet and thoughtful."

Rita's mouth dropped. Did this mean what she thought it meant? She didn't move, though. She couldn't. She wanted— no, needed—him to say it.

Reading her perfectly well, Tyler hunched his shoulders.

"I was a dick," he said without preamble. "I overreacted. I'm so used to jumping off the deep end over Randy, I blew it."

Rita's heart pounded, but she didn't say anything. She couldn't stop her bottom lip from trembling, though.

Seeing that as a minor victory, Tyler took a step closer. "I know you, Rita. You're amazing. You connect with people. You'd never hurt anyone on purpose."

She pressed her lips together, warning herself to get a grip before she started crying.

"I'm sorry I hurt you," he said. "I really am. I was so afraid of falling in love, I stopped thinking rationally."

Shock was the only thing that kept her from leaping into his arms.

Finally, he grimaced and asked, "Well? Aren't you going to say anything?"

Tears choking her voice, Rita only shook her head. Instead of words, she walked over, put her hands on either side of his chiseled cheeks and, standing on tiptoe, brushed her lips softly over his.

Tyler groaned, wrapping his arms tightly around her for a real kiss. The kind that made her head buzz and her knees melt.

"Thank you," she whispered as she pulled back.

"For?"

"For looking past the packaging. For seeing the real me, and making me see the real me, too." Rita traced the tips of her fingers over his jaw and smiled tremulously. "And for making me feel so wonderful about who I really am."

"You should," he said with a confused shrug. "You're incredible, Rita."

Which was all she needed to hear.

"I love you," she whispered.

He closed his eyes and sighed in relief.

"I love you back," he said, then he lifted her off her feet to spin her in a quick circle.

Rita giggled, throwing her head back in joy. Looked like she'd gotten the perfect Christmas gift after all.

One she never, ever, planned to return.

Epilogue

SETTING A TRAY OF COCOA-FILLED mugs on the table next to the glowing Christmas tree, Rita listened to her sisters and her parents sing to the record spinning on the glowing victrola. She wasn't sure what made her happier, the look on her parents' faces when they'd opened their gift or what it'd meant to her to give it to them.

She was a success. Not, she realized with a sigh, because she'd pulled off the best gift of the season, thanks to Tyler. But because she'd found the best gift for herself. Love. Accepting that her family loved her, that Tyler loved her. And yes, that she loved herself. It was pretty freaking awesome.

All her life, she'd been surrounded by talent and love. And she'd been so focused on what she saw as her lack of the former to appreciate the latter.

But now she knew better.

Her heart filled as she reveled in the warmth of the season and her family's love. They'd just come in from the annual living Nativity and were glowing from both joy and the chilly evening air.

"Let's drink our chocolate before it gets cold," her father decided as the record ended. "I'll go get the cookies."

"Now you girls can take a break from having Dad grill you about the new men in your lives. And give me time to come to terms with the fact that all three of you are in serious relation-ships," Amanda said with a laugh, seeing the varied looks of relief and joy on her daughters' faces. "While you wait, guess what I found when we were hauling in decorations?"

She dug behind the tree and pulled out a big floral-patterned photo box. Rita whooped and grabbed it, setting it on the couch and pulling off the lid.

"Yay. Holiday memories," she said with a smile for her mom.

"Wonderful." Layla clapped, curling up next to Rita to dig into the box of photos between them. Alison leaned over the back of the couch.

"Hey, remember this?" Alison asked, holding up a picture of the three of them in front of the bus they used to travel in. Rita grinned. Her nine-year-old self had a fashion magazine tucked under one arm. Layla's mandolin was curled in her arms like a baby, and Alison, as usual, looked perfect.

"I miss that bus," Alison said with a soft smile. Everything about her was soft tonight. Rita narrowed her eyes, wondering when she'd ever seen her sister so mellow.

"You look happy," Layla said, voicing Rita's thoughts.

"I feel happy." Alison glanced at the tree, then gave a sigh. "Like all my holiday wishes came true."

"Oh, yeah," Rita sighed. Tyler was picking her up later to take her to his mom's. Holy cow, she'd finally found a man who wanted her to meet his mother. She giggled.

"Cookies, ladies?"

Their mom took the tray from her husband and set it down before curling into his arms. "Look, Eric. It's the best Christmas ever, isn't it? Our girls, all grown-up, happy and in love."

"I'll be having a talk with their young men this week and make sure they understand just what I expect when it comes to my little girls," Eric said. His tone was joking and his smile proud, but Rita knew he wasn't kidding. He was the reason they'd all found perfect guys. Because he believed in the magic of love and everything that went with it.

Rita leaned her head against Layla's and curled her hand over Alison's where it rested on her shoulder. Smiling, they watched their parents and their wonderful example of happily ever after.

"With a love like theirs all around us," she murmured to her sisters, "how could we miss?"

* * * * *

*Harlequin Presents® is thrilled
to introduce the first installment of
an epic tale of passion and drama by*
**USA TODAY *Bestselling Author*
*Penny Jordan!***

*When buttoned-up Giselle first meets
the devastatingly handsome Saul Parenti,
the heat between them is explosive....*

"LET ME GET THIS STRAIGHT. Are you actually suggesting that I would stoop to that kind of game playing?"

Saul came out from behind his desk and walked toward her. Giselle could smell his hot male scent and it was making her dizzy, igniting a low, dull, pulsing ache that was taking over her whole body.

Giselle defended her suspicions. "You don't want me here."

"No," Saul agreed, "I don't."

And then he did what he had sworn he would not do, cursing himself beneath his breath as he reached for her, pulling her fiercely into his arms and kissing her with all the pent-up fury she had aroused in him from the moment he had first seen her.

Giselle certainly *wanted* to resist him. But the hand she raised to push him away developed a will of its own and was sliding along his bare arm beneath the sleeve of his shirt, and the body that should have been arching away from him was instead melting into him.

Beneath the pressure of his kiss he could feel and taste her gasp of undeniable response to him. He wanted to devour her, take her and drive them both until they were equally satiated—even whilst the anger within him that she should make him feel that way roared and burned its resentment of his need.

She was helpless, Giselle recognized, totally unable to withstand the storm lashing at her, able only to cling to the man who was the cause of it and pray that she would survive.

Somewhere else in the building a door banged. The sound exploded into the sensual tension that had enclosed them, driving them apart. Saul's chest was rising and falling as he fought for control; Giselle's whole body was trembling.

Without a word she turned and ran.

Find out what happens when Saul and Giselle succumb to their irresistible desire in

THE RELUCTANT SURRENDER

Available January 2011 from Harlequin Presents®

HARLEQUIN®

A *Romance*

FOR EVERY MOOD™

Spotlight on

— Classic —

Quintessential, modern love stories
that are romance at its finest.

See the next page
to enjoy a sneak peek from
the Harlequin Presents® series.

MARGARET WAY

Wealthy Australian, Secret Son

Rohan was Charlotte's shining white knight
until he disappeared—before she had
the chance to tell him she was pregnant.

But when Rohan returns years later as
a self-made millionaire, could the blond,
blue-eyed little boy and Charlotte's heart
keep him from leaving again?

Available January 2011

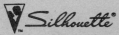

ROMANTIC

SUSPENSE

Sparked by Danger, Fueled by Passion.

NEW YORK TIMES BESTSELLING AUTHOR

RACHEL LEE

No Ordinary Hero

Strange noises...a woman's mysterious disappearance
and a killer on the loose who's too close for comfort.

With no where else to turn, Delia Carmody looks
to her aloof neighbour to help, only to discover
that Mike Windwalker is no ordinary hero.

Available in December.
Wherever books are sold.

Visit Silhouette Books at www.eHarlequin.com

SRS27709R

REQUEST YOUR FREE BOOKS!

2 FREE NOVELS
PLUS 2
FREE GIFTS!

HARLEQUIN®

Blaze™

Red-hot reads!

COMING NEXT MONTH

Available December 28, 2010